BOOKS BY MARY HIGGINS CLARK
AND CAROL HIGGINS CLARK

Deck the Halls

BOOKS BY MARY HIGGINS CLARK

On the Street Where You Live
Before I Say Good-bye
We'll Meet Again
All Through the Night
You Belong to Me
Pretend You Don't See Her
My Gal Sunday
Moonlight Becomes You
Silent Night
Let Me Call You Sweetheart
The Lottery Winner
Remember Me
I'll Be Seeing You
All Around the Town
Loves Music, Loves to Dance
The Anastasia Syndrome and Other Stories
While My Pretty One Sleeps
Weep No More, My Lady
Stillwatch
A Cry in the Night
The Cradle Will Fall
A Stranger Is Watching
Where Are the Children?

BOOKS BY CAROL HIGGINS CLARK

Fleeced
Twanged
Iced
Snagged
Decked

Mary Higgins Clark

AND

Carol Higgins Clark

He Sees You When You're Sleeping

SCRIBNER / SIMON & SCHUSTER
New York London Toronto Sydney Singapore

SCRIBNER / SIMON & SCHUSTER
1230 Avenue of the Americas
New York, NY 10020

Designed by Kyoko Watanabe
Set in Baskerville

Manufactured in the United States of America

ISBN 1-58288-146-4

Acknowledgments

It is with gratitude we acknowledge:

Our editors, Michael Korda, Chuck Adams, and Roz Lippel.

Our publicist, Lisl Cade.

Our agents, Gene Winick, Sam Pinkus, and Nick Ellison.

Our copyeditors, Associate Director of Copyediting Gypsy da Silva and copy editor Carol Catt.

Our home backup support, John Conheeney, Irene Clark, Agnes Newton, and Nadine Petry.

And, of course you, our readers.

Blessings one and all.

We dedicate this book to the victims of the September 11, 2001, tragedy,
to the families and friends who loved them,
and to the rescuers who risked their own lives to help them.

He Sees You When You're Sleeping

There's nothing worse than listening to the sounds of preparations for a great party, knowing that you're not invited. It's even worse when the party is located in heaven, Sterling Brooks thought to himself. He had been detained in the celestial waiting room, located right outside the heavenly gates, for forty-six years by earthly count. Now he could hear the heavenly choir doing a run-through of the songs that would commence the upcoming Christmas Eve celebration.

"*Hark, the herald angels sing . . .* "

Sterling sighed. He'd always loved that song. He shifted in his seat and looked around. Rows of pews were filled with people who were waiting to be called before the Heavenly Council. People who had to answer for certain things they'd done—or not done—in life, before they received admission to heaven.

Sterling had been there longer than anyone. He felt like the kid whose mother forget to pick him up from school. He usually was able to keep up a cheerful front, but lately he'd been feeling more and more forlorn. From his seat by the window, he had watched over the years as so many people he had known on earth whizzed past, on a nonstop trip to heaven. Occasionally he was shocked and a little irritated when some of them were not made to do time in the celestial waiting room. Even the guy who had cheated on his income tax and lied about his golf score soared blissfully over the bridge that separated the celestial waiting room from the heavenly gates.

But it had been the sight of Annie that tore his heart. A couple of weeks ago, the woman he'd loved but hadn't married, the woman he'd kept dangling had wafted past, looking as pretty and young as the first day they'd met. He ran to the information desk and inquired about Annie Mansfield, the soul who had just flown by the observation window. The angel checked his computer, then raised his eyebrows. "She died a few minutes ago, on her eighty-seventh birthday. While blowing out the candles, she had a dizzy spell. What an exemplary life she led. Generous. Giving. Caring. Loving."

"Did she ever marry?" Sterling asked.

The angel pressed some keys and moved the cursor, much like a ticket agent at the airport, trying to find confirmation of a reservation. He frowned. "She was engaged for a long time to some jerk who strung her along, then was heartbroken when he died unexpectedly. He was beaned in the head by a golfball." The angel pressed the cursor again and looked up at Sterling. "Oh, sorry. That's you."

Sterling slunk back to his seat. Since then he'd done a lot of thinking. He admitted to himself that he had sailed through his fifty-one years on earth, never taking on any responsibility and always managing to stay away from the unpleasant and the worrisome. I adopted Scarlett O'Hara's motto, "I'll think about it tomorrow," he acknowledged to himself.

The only time Sterling remembered experiencing prolonged anxiety was when he was on the waiting list for Brown University. All his friends from prep school had received thick envelopes from the colleges of their choice, welcoming them into the fold and strongly encouraging them to send in their checks immediately. It was only a few days before school started that he got the call from an official in the admissions office at Brown confirming that there was room for him in the freshman class. It put an end to the longest four and a half months of his life.

He knew that the reason he had only squeaked into Brown was that, although he was blessed with a keen intelligence and excellent all-around athletic skills, he had simply coasted through high school.

A chill that was pure fear engulfed him. He'd finally gotten into the college he wanted, but maybe up here he wouldn't be so fortunate. Until right now he had been absolutely sure that he'd make it to heaven. Sterling had reminded the angel at the door to the Heavenly Council that some of the people who came in behind him had been called and suggested that perhaps he had been inadvertently overlooked. He had been told politely but firmly to return to his seat.

He so much wanted to be in heaven this Christmas Eve. The expression on the faces of the people who soared past the window, seeing the open gates ahead of them, had filled him with wonder. And now Annie was there.

The angel at the door signaled for everyone's attention. "I have glad tidings. Christmas amnesty has been granted to the following. You will not have to appear before the Heavenly Council. You will go straight through the exit door on the right that leads directly to the heavenly bridge. Stand and file through in an orderly fashion as your name is called . . . Walter Cummings . . ."

A few pews over, Walter, a sprightly ninety-year-old, jumped up and clicked his heels together. "Hallelujah!" he shouted as he ran to the front of the room.

"I said in an orderly fashion," the angel chided in a somewhat resigned voice. "Though I can't much blame you," he murmured as he called the next name. "Tito Ortiz . . ."

Tito whooped with joy and raced down the aisle, hot on Walter's heels.

"Jackie Mills, Dennis Pines, Veronica Murphy, Charlotte Green, Pasquale D'Amato, Winthrop Lloyd III, Charlie Potters, Jacob Weiss, Ten Eyck Elmendorf . . ."

Name after name after name was called as the pews emptied out.

The angel finished reading from the list and folded the paper. Sterling was the only one left. A tear formed in his eye. The celestial waiting room felt cavernous and lonely. I must have been a terrible person, he thought. I'm not going to make it to heaven after all.

The angel laid down the list and began to walk toward him. Oh no, Sterling thought frantically, don't tell me he's sending me to the other place. For the first time, he realized what it was like to feel completely helpless and hopeless.

"Sterling Brooks," the angel said. "You have been summoned to an extraordinary meeting of the Heavenly Council. Follow me, please."

A tiny whisper of hope flickered in Sterling's being. Maybe, just maybe, he still had a chance. Bracing himself, he stood up and followed the angel to the door of the chamber. The angel, his face and voice full of sympathy, whispered, "Good luck," as he opened the door and pushed Sterling inside.

The room was not large. It was bathed in a soft, exquisite light, the likes of which Sterling had never experienced. The floor-to-ceiling window gave an awesome view of the heavenly gates and he realized the light was reflecting off them.

Four men and four women were seated at a long table, facing him. From the halos shining around their heads, he realized immediately that they were all saints, even though he didn't recognize them from the stained-glass windows in cathedrals he had visited while on vacation. The outfits they were wearing varied from biblical robes to twentieth-century dress. With the instinctive knowledge that was now part of him, Sterling understood that they were wearing the typical garb of the periods in which they had lived. The man at the far end, a grave-faced monk, opened the proceedings.

"Sit down, Sterling. We've got a bone to pick with you."

Sterling took the seat, acutely aware that all eyes were fixed on him.

One of the women, dressed in an elegant red velvet gown

and wearing a tiara, said in a cultured voice, "You had an easy life, didn't you, Sterling?"

Looks like you did too, Sterling thought, but held his tongue. He nodded meekly. "Yes, ma'am."

The monk looked at him sternly. "Uneasy lies the head that wears a crown. Her majesty did great good for her subjects."

My God, they can read my thoughts, Sterling realized, and he began to tremble.

"But you never went out of your way for anybody," the queen continued.

"You were a fair-weather friend," said a man in shepherd's garb, seated second from the right.

"Passive-aggressive," declared a young matador, who was picking a thread off the end of his red cape.

"What does that mean?" Sterling asked, frightened.

"Oh, sorry. That earthly expression came into use after your time. It's a very popular one now, believe me."

"Covers a multitude of sins," muttered a beautiful woman who reminded Sterling of the pictures he'd seen of Pocahontas.

"Aggressive?" Sterling said. "I never lost my temper. Ever."

"Passive-aggressive is something different. You hurt people by *not* doing things. And by making promises you have no intention of keeping."

"You were self-absorbed," a sweet-faced nun on the end said. "You were a good estate lawyer, tidying up little problems for the ultrarich, but you never lent your expertise to the poor unfortunate who was unfairly losing his home or the lease on his store. What's worse, you actually considered helping out once in a while and then decided not to get involved." She shook her head. "You were too much of a good-time Charlie."

"The kind who jumped into the first lifeboat when the ship was going down," a saint in the uniform of a British admiral snapped. "A cad, by George. Why, you never once helped an old lady cross the street."

"I never once spotted an old lady who needed help!"

"That's it in a nutshell," they said in unison. "You were too smug and self-absorbed to really notice what was going on around you."

"I'm sorry," Sterling said humbly. "I thought I was a pretty nice guy. I never meant to hurt anybody. Is there anything I can do now to make it up?"

The members of the council looked at each other.

"How bad could I have been?" Sterling cried. He pointed toward the waiting room. "In all this time I've talked to a lot of the souls who have passed through there. None of them were saints! And by the way, I saw someone who cheated on his income tax go straight to heaven. You must have missed him!"

They all laughed. "You're absolutely right. We were on a coffee break. But on the other hand, he donated a lot of that money to charity."

"What about his golf game?" Sterling asked eagerly. "I never once cheated the way he did. And I got hit in the head by a golf ball. As I was dying, I forgave the guy who did it. Not everyone would be that nice."

They stared at him as his mind filled with images of all the times in his life when he'd let people down. Annie. He was too selfish to marry her, but he always let her keep hoping because he didn't want to lose her. After he died, it was too late for her to have the family she always wanted. And now she was in heaven. He had to see her again.

Sterling felt wretched. He had to know his fate. "What are you telling me?" he asked. "Will I ever get to heaven?"

"Funny you should ask," the monk replied. "We've discussed your case, and we've decided that you seem to be the appropriate candidate for an experiment we've been weighing for some time."

Sterling's ears pricked up. All was not lost.

"I love experiments," he said enthusiastically. "I'm your boy. Try me. When do we start?" He realized he was starting to sound like a jerk.

"Sterling, be quiet and listen. You are being sent back to earth. It is your job to recognize someone with a problem and help that person solve it."

"Sent back to earth!" Sterling was dumbfounded.

The eight heads nodded in unison.

"How long will I stay?"

"As long as it takes to solve the problem."

"Does that mean if I do a good job I'll be allowed to enter heaven? I'd love to be there for Christmas."

They all looked amused. "Not so fast," the monk said. "In the jargon of the day, you have a lot of frequent flier miles to earn before you achieve permanent residence inside those holy gates. However, if you complete your first mission to our satisfaction by Christmas Eve, you will be entitled to a visitor's pass for twenty-four hours."

Sterling's heart sank a little. Oh well, he thought. Every long journey begins with one small step.

"You'd do well to remember that," the queen cautioned.

Sterling blinked. He'd have to remember they were mind readers. "How will I know the person I'm supposed to help?" he asked.

"That's part of the point of this experiment. You have to learn to recognize people's needs and do something about them," a young black woman wearing a nurse's uniform told him.

"Will I have any help? I mean, anyone I can talk to if I'm not sure what to do? I'll do anything to get the job done properly, you understand."

I'm babbling again, he thought.

"You are free at any time to request a consultation with us," the admiral assured him.

"When do I start?"

The monk pressed a button on the council table. "Right now."

Sterling felt a trap door open beneath him. In an instant he was hurtling past the stars, around the moon, through the clouds, and then suddenly whisking past a tall, brilliantly lit Christmas tree. His feet touched the earth.

"My God," Sterling breathed. "I'm in Rockefeller Center."

Marissa's dark hair cascaded around her shoulders as she twirled around the rink in Rockefeller Center. She had started taking ice-skating lessons when she was three. Now that she was seven, skating was as natural to her as breathing, and lately it had been the only thing that eased the hurt that filled her chest and throat.

The music changed, and without thinking she adjusted to the new, softer rhythm, a waltz. For a moment she pretended she was with Daddy. She could almost feel his hand linked with hers, could almost see NorNor, her grandmother, smiling at her.

Then she remembered that she really didn't want to skate with Daddy or even talk to him, or to NorNor. They had gone away, hardly saying good-bye to her. The first bunch of times they phoned she had pleaded with them to come back or to let her come visit them, but they had said that was impossible. Now when they called, she wouldn't talk to them.

She didn't care, she told herself.

But still, she closed her eyes whenever a car she was in happened to drive past NorNor's restaurant; it hurt to remember how much fun it had been to go there with Daddy. The place was always crowded, sometimes NorNor played the piano, and people always asked Daddy to sing. Sometimes they'd bring over his CD and ask him to sign the cover.

Now she never went there. She had heard Mommy tell Roy—he was Mommy's husband now—that without NorNor, the restaurant was really struggling and would probably have to close soon.

What did Daddy and NorNor expect when they went away? Marissa wondered. NorNor always said that unless she was there every night the place would fall on its face. "It's my living room," she used to tell Marissa. "You don't invite people over to your house and not be there."

If NorNor loved her restaurant so much, why did she go away? And if Daddy and NorNor loved *her* like they said, why did they leave her behind?

She hadn't seen them in almost a whole year. Christmas Eve was her birthday. She would be eight years old, and even though she still was very angry with them, she had promised God that if the bell rang on Christmas Eve and they were standing at the door, she would never be mean to anyone as long as she lived and would help Mommy with the babies and stop acting bored when Roy told the same stupid stories over and over. If it would help, she'd even promise never to skate again as long as she lived, but she knew that was a promise Daddy wouldn't want her to make, because if he ever *did* come back, he'd want to take her skating.

The music stopped and the skating teacher, Miss Carr, who had brought twelve students to Rockefeller Center as a special treat, motioned that it was time to go. Marissa did one final pirouette before she coasted to the exit. The minute she started to untie her laces the hurt came back. She could feel it growing around her heart and filling her chest and then rising like a tide into her throat. But though it was a struggle, she managed to keep it from pressing against her eyes.

"You're a terrific skater," one of the attendants said. "You'll be a star like Tara Lipinsky when you grow up."

NorNor used to tell her that all the time. Before she could help herself, Marissa's eyes began to blur. Turning her head so that the attendant wouldn't see that she was almost crying, she looked straight into the eyes of a man who was standing at the fence around the rink. He was wearing a funny-looking hat and coat, but he had a nice face and he was sort of smiling at her.

"Come along, Marissa," Miss Carr called, and Marissa, hearing the slightly grouchy tone in her teacher's voice, began to run to catch up with the other kids.

"It seems familiar and yet so different," Sterling murmured to himself as he glanced around Rockefeller Center. For one thing it was far more crowded than the last time he was here. Every inch of space seemed to be filled with people. Some were carrying shopping bags laden with gifts, hurrying about, while others stood gazing up at the big tree.

This tree seemed taller than the last one he had seen here—forty-six years ago—and it had more lights on it than he remembered. It was magnificent, but so different from the otherworldly light he had experienced in the celestial conference room.

Even though he'd grown up on Seventieth Street off Fifth Avenue, and lived most of his life in Manhattan, a sudden wave of homesickness for the celestial life swept over him. He needed to find the person he was supposed to help so he could complete his mission.

Two young children came racing toward him. He stepped aside before they ran into him, then realized he had bumped into a woman who was admiring the tree.

"I beg your pardon," he said. "I hope I didn't hurt you?" She did not look at him or indicate that she had heard a single word he said, or even that she'd felt the bump.

She doesn't know I'm here, he realized. He had a moment of total dismay. How can I help someone if that person can't see or hear me? he wondered. The council really left me to sink or swim on my own.

Sterling looked into the faces of the passersby. They were talking to each other, laughing, carrying packages, pointing to the tree. No one seemed to be in any special distress. He thought of how the admiral said he never helped an old lady cross the street. Maybe he should try to find one now.

He walked quickly toward Fifth Avenue and was appalled at the volume of traffic he saw. He passed a shop window, then stopped, astonished when he saw his reflection gazing back at him. Other people couldn't see him, but he could see himself. He studied his image in the window. Not bad, old boy, he thought admiringly. It was the first time he'd seen his reflection since that fateful morning when he left for the golf course. He noted his salt-and-pepper hair, in the early stages of recession, his somewhat angular features, his lean, muscular body. He was wearing his winter outerwear: a dark blue chesterfield coat with a velvet collar, his favorite hat, a gray felt homburg, and gray kidskin gloves. Noticing the way other people were dressed, he realized that his clothing must have gone out of style.

If people could see me, they'd think I was heading for a costume party, he decided.

At Fifth Avenue, he looked uptown. His best friend used to

work at American President Lines. The office was gone. He was aware that many of the shops and firms that he remembered had been replaced. Well, it *has* been forty-six years, he thought. Now, where is the sweet old lady who requires assistance?

It was almost as though the council had heard him. An elderly woman with a cane began crossing the street as the light was turning red. That's too dangerous, he thought, even though the traffic was barely crawling.

Taking long strides, he rushed to assist her, but was chagrined to see that a young man had recognized her plight and was already grabbing her elbow.

"Leave me alone," she screamed. "I've gotten by for a long time without the likes of you trying to grab my pocketbook."

The young man muttered something under his breath, dropped her arm, and left her in the middle of the street. Horns blared, but the traffic stopped as, without any indication of haste, the old lady made her way to the curb.

Clearly the council didn't send me back to earth for her, Sterling decided.

There was a long line in front of the Saks Fifth Avenue windows. He wondered what they were looking at that was so special. Nothing but clothes was ever displayed in those windows, he thought. From the corner of his eye he could see the spires of Saint Patrick's Cathedral, and he felt his sense of urgency deepen.

Let's reason this out, he thought. I was sent to help someone, and I was placed in Rockefeller Center. That certainly suggests that I'm supposed to begin my task there. Sterling turned and retraced his steps.

With ever-increasing care he studied the faces of the people he was passing. A couple walked by, both wearing skintight, black leather outfits, both also appearing to have been scalped. Pierced noses and eyebrows completed the fashion statement. He tried not to stare. Times sure have changed, he thought.

As he moved through the crowd, he sensed he was being drawn back toward the majestic Christmas tree that was the heart of the holiday season at Rockefeller Center.

He found himself standing next to a more traditional looking young couple, holding hands and appearing to be very much in love. He felt like an eavesdropper, but he had to hear what they were saying. Something made him certain the young man was about to propose. Go for it, he thought. Before it's too late.

"I've decided it's time," the young man said.

"I'm ready too." The girl's eyes were shining.

Where's the ring? Sterling wondered.

"We'll move in together for six months and see how it works out."

The young woman looked blissful. "I'm so happy," she whispered.

Shaking his head, Sterling turned away. That was never an option in my time, he told himself. Somewhat discouraged, he walked to the railing overlooking the ice-skating rink and looked down. The music was just ending, and skaters were heading for the exit. He saw one little girl give a final twirl. She's very good, he thought admiringly.

A moment later she looked up, and he could see that she was trying to blink back tears. Their eyes locked. Does she see me? Sterling wondered. He couldn't be sure, but he was certain that she had sensed his presence, and that she needed him. As he watched her slowly skate off the ice, her shoulders drooping noticeably, he knew with certainty that she was the one he had been sent to help.

He watched as she changed into her shoes and then headed up the stairs from the rink. He momentarily lost her in the crowd, but then caught up with her just as she was boarding a van marked MADISON VILLAGE SCHOOLS that was waiting on Forty-ninth Street. So that's where they were going, he thought—Long Island. He heard the teacher call his new little charge Marissa. Obviously the youngest student in the group, she went straight to the back and sat alone in the last seat. Quickly becoming comfortable in the knowledge that no one could see him, he followed the little girl onto the van and slid into the seat across the aisle from her. She glanced in his direction several times, as if she somehow were aware that he was there.

Sterling settled back. He was on his way. He looked over at Marissa, who had leaned against the window and closed her eyes. What was weighing so heavily on that little girl's heart? Who was she thinking about?

He couldn't wait to see what was going on in her home.

"I can't believe it. Another Christmas with Mama so many miles away." Eddie Badgett was close to tears. "I miss my homeland. I miss my mama. I want to see her."

His ruddy face dissolved in grief. He ran his thick fingers through his plentiful grizzled hair.

The Yuletide season had thrown Eddie into a blue funk that all his worldly wealth, accumulated through loan-sharking and pyramid schemes, could not erase.

He was speaking to his brother Junior, who, at fifty-four, was three years younger. Junior had been named for their father, who had spent most of his sons' lives incarcerated in a dank prison cell in Wallonia, a tiny country bordering Albania.

The brothers were in the room their pricey decorator had grandly dubbed the library, and which he had filled with books that neither one of them had any intention of reading.

The Badgetts' mansion, set on twelve acres on Long Island's North Shore gold coast, was a tribute to the ability of the brothers to separate other human beings from their hard-earned assets.

Their lawyer, Charlie Santoli, was with them in the library, seated at the ornate marble table, his briefcase beside him, an open file in front of him.

Santoli, a small, neat, sixtyish man with the unfortunate tendency to complete his daily toilette with a substantial quantity of Manly Elegance cologne, eyed the brothers with his usual combination of disdain and fear.

It frequently occurred to him that in appearance the pair resembled a bowling ball and a baseball bat. Eddie was short, squat, rounded, hard. Junior was tall, lean, powerful. And sinister—he could chill a room with his smile or even the grin he considered ingratiating.

Charlie's mouth was dry. It was his unhappy duty to tell the brothers that he'd been unable to get another postponement of their trial for racketeering, loan-sharking, arson, and attempted murder. Which meant that Billy Campbell, the handsome, thirty-year-old, climbing-the-charts rock singer, and his glamorous mother, aging cabaret singer and popular restaurant owner Nor Kelly, would be whisked out of hiding and brought to federal court. Their testimony would put Eddie and Junior in prison cells that they could cover with pictures of Mama, because they'd never lay eyes on her again. But Santoli knew that, even from prison, they would manage to make sure that Billy Campbell never sang another note, and that his mother, Nor Kelly, never welcomed another patron to her restaurant.

"You're too scared to talk to us," Junior barked. "But you'd better start. We're all ears."

"Yeah," Eddie echoed, as he dabbed his eyes and blew his nose, "we're all ears."

Madison Village was a few exits past Syosset on the Long Island Expressway.

At the school parking lot, Sterling followed Marissa off the van. Wet snowflakes swirled around them. A guy in his late thirties, with thinning sandy hair—tall, lanky, the kind Sterling's mother would describe as "a long drink of water"—called to Marissa and waved vigorously.

"Over here, honey pie. Hurry. No hat on? You'll catch a cold."

Sterling heard Marissa groan as she ran toward a beige sedan parked in the midst of a half-dozen vehicles that looked to Sterling more like trucks than cars. He had noticed a lot of this kind of vehicle on the highway. He shrugged. Just another change in the last forty-six years.

Marissa said, "Hi, Roy," as she hopped into the front seat. Sterling squeezed himself into the back between two tiny seats that were obviously for very small children. What will they think of next? Sterling wondered. When I was a toddler, my mother used to drive with me in her lap and let me help her steer.

"How's our little Olympic skater?" Roy asked Marissa. Sterling could tell he was trying his best to be pleasant, but Marissa wasn't having any of it.

"Good," she replied without a trace of enthusiasm.

Who is this guy? Sterling wondered. It can't be her father. Maybe an uncle? The mother's boyfriend?

"Fasten your seat belt, princess," Roy cautioned in a too-cheery voice.

Honey pie? Princess? Olympic skater? This guy is embarrassing, Sterling thought.

Give me a break, Marissa sighed.

Startled, Sterling looked for Roy's reaction. There was none. Roy was staring straight ahead, paying rapt attention to the road. His hands were wrapped tightly around the steering wheel, and he was driving ten miles below the speed limit.

I could skate home faster, Marissa moaned.

Sterling was inordinately pleased to realize that he not only had the power to make himself visible to her on demand, but when he tuned in, he could read her thoughts as well. The Heavenly Council was obviously making certain tools and powers available to him, but leaving it up to him to discover their extent. They certainly weren't going to make it easy for him.

He leaned back, aware that even though he was not there in the flesh, he nonetheless felt crowded and uncomfortable. He had had much the same reaction when he'd bumped into the woman at the skating rink.

The rest of the seven-minute ride home was spent mostly

in silence, except for the radio, which was tuned to a station playing particularly bland music.

Marissa remembered the time she had switched the station in Daddy's car to the one that played this stuff. He had said, "You're kidding! Haven't I given you any taste in music?"

"This is the station Roy listens to!" Marissa had cried triumphantly. They had laughed together.

"How your mother went from me to him I'll never know," Daddy had marveled.

So that's it, Sterling thought. Roy is her stepfather. But where's her father, and why, now that she's thought about him, is she both sad and angry?

"Roy went to pick her up. They should be here any minute, but I don't think she'll want to talk to you, Billy. I've tried to explain that it isn't your fault that you and Nor have to stay away for a while, but she isn't buying it." Denise Ward was on her cordless phone, talking to Marissa's father, her ex-husband, and trying to keep her two-year-old twin boys from pulling down the Christmas tree.

"I understand, but it's killing me that—"

"Roy Junior, let go of that tinsel!" Denise interrupted, her voice rising. "Robert, leave the baby Jesus alone. I said . . . Hold on, Billy."

Two thousand miles away, Billy Campbell's concerned expression cleared for a moment. He was holding up the receiver so that his mother, Nor Kelly, could hear the conversation. Now he raised his eyebrows. "I think the baby Jesus just went flying across the room," he whispered.

"Sorry, Billy," Denise said, back on the phone. "Look, it's pretty hectic here. The munchkins are all excited about Christmas. Maybe you'd better call back in fifteen minutes, even though it's going to be a waste of time. Marissa just doesn't want to talk to either you or Nor."

"Denise, I know you've got your hands full," Billy Campbell said quietly. "You have the packages we sent, but is there anything Marissa really needs? Maybe she's talked about something special I could still get for her."

He heard a loud crash and the sound of a wailing two-year-old.

"Oh my God, the Waterford angel," Denise Ward nearly sobbed. "Don't go near it, Robert. Do you hear me? You'll get cut." Her voice taut with anger, she snapped, "You want to know what Marissa needs, Billy? She needs you and Nor, and she needs both of you soon. I'm worried sick about her. Roy is too. He tries so hard with her, and she simply won't respond."

"How do you think I feel, Denise?" Billy asked, his voice rising. "I'd give my right arm to be with Marissa. My guts are torn out every day that I'm not with her. I'm grateful that Roy is there for her, but she's my kid and I miss her."

"I think of how lucky I am to have met a dependable man who has a nice steady job, who isn't out till all hours playing with a rock group, and doesn't get himself into situations where he has to hightail it out of town." Denise did not pause for breath. "Marissa is hurting. Have you got that, Billy? Her birthday is in four days. Christmas Eve. I don't know what she'll be like when you're not here for that. The child feels abandoned."

Nor Kelly saw the expression of pain that came over her son's face and watched as he clasped his hand over his forehead. Her ex-daughter-in-law was a good mother, but was nearing the end of her rope out of frustration with the situation. She wanted them back for Marissa's sake, but would be frantic with worry that Marissa might be in danger if they were around.

"So, Billy, I'll tell her you called. I've got to hang up. Oh, wait a minute. The car just pulled into the driveway. I'll see if she'll talk to you."

A nice house, Sterling thought as he followed Marissa and Roy up the steps. Tudor style. Evergreens covered with blue lights. A small sleigh with Santa and the eight reindeer on the lawn. Everything pristine. He was sure Roy was a neatnik.

Roy unlocked the door and flung it open. "Where are my munchkins?" he called playfully. "Roy Junior, Robert, your daddy's back."

Sterling jumped aside as two identical sandy-haired toddlers raced toward them. He could see into the living room where a pretty blond woman, looking extremely harried, was holding a phone with no cord (obviously another innovation since Sterling's departure). She gestured to Marissa. "Your dad and NorNor want to talk to you very, very much," she said.

Marissa walked into the living room, took the phone from her mother, and to Sterling's astonishment, replaced the receiver on the cradle, and, her eyes brimming with tears, ran upstairs.

Wow! Sterling thought.

He didn't yet know what the problem was, but he empathized with the helpless glance Marissa's mother exchanged with her husband. It looks as though I've got my work cut out for me, he decided. Marissa needs help *now.*

He followed Marissa up the stairs and knocked on the door of her room.

"Please leave me alone, Mom. I'm not hungry, and I don't want to eat."

"It's not Mom, Marissa," Sterling said.

He heard the lock turn, and the door opened slowly. Marissa's eyes widened, and her woebegone expression changed to one of astonishment. "I saw you when I was skating and then when I got in the van," she whispered. "But then I didn't see you anymore. Are you a ghost?"

Sterling smiled at her. "Not really a ghost. I'm more on the order of an angel, but I'm not really an angel. In fact that's why I'm here."

"You want to help me, don't you?"

Sterling felt a wrench of tenderness as he looked into Marissa's troubled blue eyes. "I want to help you more than anything in the world. For my sake as well as yours."

"Are you in trouble with God?"

"Let's just say he's not thrilled with me at the moment. He doesn't think I'm ready for heaven yet."

Marissa rolled her eyes. "I know lots of people who are never going to get to heaven."

Sterling laughed. "There were some people I was sure wouldn't make it, and now they're right up there with the best of them."

"Go figure," Marissa said. "Do you want to come in? I have a chair that was big enough for my dad when he came over to help me with my homework."

She's charming, Sterling thought as he followed her into the spacious room. What a little personality. He was glad that Marissa knew instinctively that he was a kindred spirit, one she could trust. She already looked a little happier.

He settled himself in the armchair she indicated and realized he was still wearing his hat. "Oh, sorry," he murmured, took it off, and placed it neatly on his lap.

Marissa pulled out her desk chair and sat down with the air of a polite hostess. "I wish I could offer you a soda and some cookies or something, but if I go downstairs they'll want me to eat dinner." She wrinkled her nose. "I just thought about something. Do you get hungry? Can you eat? Because it looks like you're there, but not really."

"I'm just trying to figure all that out myself," Sterling admitted. "This is my first shot at this sort of thing. Now tell me, why won't you talk to your dad?"

Marissa looked down as a shadow fell over her face. "He won't come and see me and he won't let me go and visit him and neither will NorNor—she's my grandmother. And if they don't want to see me, I don't want to see them."

"Where do they live?"

"I don't know," Marissa burst out. "They won't tell me, and Mom doesn't know. She said they're hiding out from bad people who want to hurt them and they can't come back until it's safe, but at school kids say they think Daddy and NorNor got in trouble and had to run away."

Which is it? Sterling wondered. "When was the last time you saw them?"

"Two days after Christmas last year was when I *really* saw them. Daddy and I went ice skating. Then we went back to NorNor's restaurant for lunch. We were supposed to go to Radio City Music Hall on New Year's Eve morning, but he and NorNor had to go away. They rushed in when I was hardly even awake and said good-bye. They didn't tell me when they were coming back, and it's been almost a whole year." She paused. "I have to see Daddy, I have to see NorNor."

Her heart is broken, Sterling thought. He understood that kind of ache. It was like the yearning he felt when he saw Annie go past the window to heaven.

"Marissa . . ." There was a knock at the bedroom door.

"Oh, I knew it," Marissa said. "Mom is going to make me go down and have dinner. I'm not hungry and I don't want you to leave."

"Marissa, I'm going to get to work on your problem. I'll be back to say good night."

"Promise?"

"Marissa." There was another knock at the door.

"Yes, but you promise me something in return," Sterling said hastily. "Your mom is really worried about you. Give her a break."

"Okay. I'll even give Roy a break, and anyhow, I like chicken. Mom, I'm coming," she called. She turned back to Sterling. "Give me a high five."

"What's that?" Sterling asked.

Marissa was incredulous. "You must be pretty old. Everybody knows what a high five is."

"I've been out of touch," Sterling admitted as, following her example, he raised his hand, palm flat, and held it open as she gave it an enthusiastic slap.

Precocious, he thought, smiling. "See you later," he whispered.

"Great. Don't forget your hat. I don't want to be mean, but it really looks dumb."

"Marissa, dinner's getting cold," her mother called.

"Dinner's always cold," Marissa whispered to Sterling as he walked her to the door. "Roy takes forever to say grace. Daddy says Mommy should stick to cold cuts."

Her hand was on the knob. "Mommy can't see you, can she?"

Sterling shook his head and disappeared.

In the celestial conference room, the board had been following Sterling's movements with interest. "He's made contact immediately. Using the old noggin, I call it," the admiral said approvingly.

"That little girl is so unhappy," the nun said softly.

"And quite outspoken," the monk observed. "However, I do realize it was different in my day. Sterling is about to request a conference with us. I believe we should grant it."

"So be it," they chorused.

Deep in thought, Sterling stood for a brief time in the breezeway of Marissa's home, sheltered from the slowly falling snow. I could snoop around town and find out about her father and grandmother, he thought, but there's an easier way to get the full picture, one that would involve requesting permission from the council.

He closed his eyes. Before he even had time to make the request, he found himself in the conference room. Relieved, he saw from their faces that his saintly mentors seemed to be observing him with guarded favor.

"I see you tried to find an old lady in distress," the admiral chuckled. "The young fellow who beat you to her got quite a surprise. I say, she was a prickly one."

"At least Sterling didn't waste a minute when he reached earth," the nurse said approvingly.

Sterling glowed to hear the praise. "Thank you, thank you. As you can understand, I don't want to waste a minute now. I believe I can best help Marissa when I fully understand the cause of her problem.

"Marissa's father and grandmother were planning to take her to Radio City Music Hall last New Year's Eve morning. But something went wrong just before that. They came to see her very early that day and told her they had to go away for a while."

The monk nodded. "To get to the root of most problems you have to do some digging in the past."

The shepherd, who had been very quiet, suddenly spoke up. "Most people's problems go way back. You should have met my family. Why do you think I became a shepherd? The only place I got a little peace was out on the hill."

They all laughed. "Don't get me started," the queen said. "My family's problems were the talk of the kingdom."

The monk cleared his throat. "I think we all understand you, Sterling. We know why you're here. You are requesting permission to go back in time to learn why Marissa's father and grandmother needed to leave town."

"That's it, sir," Sterling said humbly. "Perhaps you feel

that by granting permission you'll make my job too easy, and of course, if that's the case, I don't expect special favors."

"When you see what this is all about you may need a few special favors," the matador said wryly. "Personally, it's my opinion that you'll be stepping in the ring with two bulls, not one, and—"

The monk shushed the matador. "It is Sterling's job to figure this out for himself." His hand reached for the button.

That was fast, Sterling thought as he felt himself once again hurtling through the solar system. They're sending me a different way. I guess because I'm going back in time.

The next thing he knew he was standing in the parking lot of an inviting-looking restaurant. Seems to be pretty popular, he observed. Through the windows he could see that there was a bustle of activity inside. To get his bearings, he walked to the end of the driveway and read the sign: NOR'S PLACE.

Very good, he thought. Marissa's grandmother's restaurant. He didn't need to be Sherlock Holmes to figure out that the next step would be to go inside and take a look around. He hurried back up the driveway, climbed the steps, crossed the porch, and started to open the door.

I can just go through it, he chided himself. No use wasting heat. A sharp breeze accompanied him inside, where a shapely woman of about sixty, with blond hair held up in a loose twist by a jeweled comb, was standing at a small desk, studying the reservations book.

She looked up. Tendrils of blond hair brushed her forehead.

A most attractive woman in a showy kind of way, Sterling thought.

"I'd swear I shut that door tight," Nor Kelly murmured as with two quick strides she was beside him, giving the door a decisive pull.

"NorNor, sit down. Your coffee's here," a child's voice called.

A familiar voice. Sterling whirled around to face the dining room. Mahogany paneled walls, tables covered with crisp white cloths and topped with wide red candles created a cheery and welcoming atmosphere. A piano was at a right angle to the bar. Strings of Christmas lights twinkled on the walls and windows, and holiday music was playing softly in the background.

"NorNor," the child called again.

His eyes roamed the crowded room. A little girl was standing at a corner table just to the right of the door. She was looking in his direction. It was Marissa! She was slightly younger looking, her hair a little shorter, but the most noticeable difference was how happy she looked. Her eyes were sparkling, her lips were curved in a smile, she had on a bright red skating outfit. With her was a strikingly handsome, blue-eyed, dark-haired man in his late twenties.

Billy Campbell, Sterling thought. He's got movie-star looks. I wish I'd looked like that when I was alive, he reflected. Not that I had anything to complain about.

Nor looked up. "I'll be right there, Rissa."

It was obvious Marissa had not seen him. Of course, Sterling thought. We're not due to meet until next year.

He strolled over to the table and took a seat opposite Marissa. What a difference in her, he thought tenderly.

She and her father were finishing lunch. The crusts of a grilled cheese sandwich were on Marissa's plate. I never liked crusts either, Sterling remembered.

"Daddy, can't I please go to the party with you?" Marissa asked as she played with the straw in her soda. "I love to hear you and NorNor sing, and I promise I won't be a pest."

"You're never a pest, Rissa," Billy said, giving her hair a tug. "But this party is not for kids, believe me."

"I want to see what that big house looks like inside."

"A lot of people do," Billy murmured, raising one eyebrow. "Listen, we're going to Radio City on New Year's Eve. That will be a lot more fun. Trust me."

"A kid at school said that the men who own that house are like the people in *The Sopranos.*"

Billy laughed. "That's another reason not to bring you there, kiddo."

Sopranos? Sterling thought.

Nor Kelly slipped into the chair next to Marissa. "Don't forget your other grandma is coming to your mom's house in time for dinner tonight. You were looking forward to seeing her."

"She's staying for three days. I can see her tomorrow. I don't want to miss the chance to hear you two sing."

Billy's eyes twinkled. "You're too young to be a groupie."

Groupie? So many new words, Sterling thought.

"Daddy, everybody loves your new song. You're going to be so famous."

"You bet he is, Rissa," Nor confirmed.

I can see why Marissa has missed them so much, Sterling thought. She's in her element with them. Already, he thoroughly liked Nor Kelly and Billy Campbell. You could not mistake that they were mother and son, and that Marissa had inherited those blue eyes, fair skin, and good looks from them. Nor and Billy had the natural charisma of born performers, and Marissa was already showing signs of possessing that same quality.

The restaurant was beginning to empty, and people were stopping by the table to say good-bye. "See you on New Year's Eve," a number of them said. "We'd never miss your party, Nor."

"That party I'm coming to," Marissa said decisively, pointing her finger for emphasis.

"Until ten o'clock," Billy agreed, "then you're out of here."

"Don't try last year's trick of hiding behind the bar when it's time to go home," Nor warned, laughing. "And speaking of going home, your mother should be here any minute, and Daddy and I have to get moving. We're due at our job in an hour."

Billy stood up. "Here's Mom, Rissa."

Denise Ward was crossing the room to them. "Hi, Billy. Hi, Nor. I'm sorry I'm late," she apologized. "I had to pick up some groceries, and the line at the checkout counter practically went around the store. But I bought what we need to make cookies, Marissa."

Neither Denise nor Billy could be thirty yet, Sterling thought. They obviously had married young, and although divorced, seemed to have stayed friendly. Just looking at the two of them, she in her somewhat prim winter pantsuit and he in his black jeans and boots, you could tell they weren't on the same wavelength.

And God knows Billy Campbell hadn't followed the adage that every man marries his mother. No one would ever accuse Nor Kelly of looking prim. She was wearing a striking white cashmere pantsuit with a colorful print silk scarf, complemented by eye-catching costume jewelry.

"How are the babies?" Nor asked.

"Just starting to walk," Denise announced proudly. "When Roy Junior took his first step, Roy Senior stayed up half the night, installing gates all over the house."

Sterling thought he detected a slight roll of Billy's eyes. She's letting Billy know how helpful Roy is, Sterling decided. I bet he hears about some new accomplishment of Roy's every time he sees her.

Marissa stood up and hugged her father and grandmother. "Have fun with the Sopranos," she said.

Denise looked surprised. "The Sopranos?"

"She's joking," Nor said hastily. "Our job this evening is at the party the Badgett brothers are giving to benefit the senior citizens center."

"Don't they live in that big house—?" Denise began.

"Yes, they do," Marissa blurted, "and I hear they have an indoor pool and a bowling alley."

"We'll let you know every sorry detail," Billy promised. "Come on. Let's get your jacket."

As they started walking toward the coat check, Sterling took a moment to look at the framed photos along the walls. Many of them showed Nor posing with diners at the tables. Some were autographed by people who were probably present-day celebrities, he decided. There were pictures of a glamorous Nor onstage, singing with a band; Billy, guitar in hand, performing with a group; Nor and Billy together onstage; Billy and Nor with Marissa.

Sterling could see from the older pictures that Nor once must have been a cabaret singer. He came upon a number of photographs in which she was performing with a partner. The sign on the bandstand read NOR KELLY AND BILL CAMPBELL. Billy's father, Sterling thought. I wonder what happened to him, and how long has she had the restaurant? Then a poster for a New Year's Eve celebration at Nor's Place dating back twenty years made him realize that she had been in this business a long time.

Marissa left after a final kiss from Billy and Nor. Even though Sterling knew that Marissa couldn't see him, he felt left out that she hadn't somehow sensed his presence and maybe given him a high five.

You're being ridiculous, he chided himself. But when he saw Marissa with Billy it made him think of the child he might have had if he and Annie had married.

Agreeing to be ready to leave in fifteen minutes, Billy and Nor rushed to change. To kill time, Sterling wandered over to the bar, where a single patron was chatting with the bartender. He sat on a nearby stool. If I were still alive, I'd order a scotch, he thought. It's certainly been a long time since I had one. Next year Marissa will ask me if I get hungry or thirsty. Actually, I don't have any desire to eat or drink, he realized, even though I get cold when I'm outside and feel crowded in cars. As Marissa would say, "Go figure."

"Christmas was nice, Dennis," the patron was saying. "I never thought I'd get through it, the first one without Peggy. Honest to God, when I went downstairs that morning I was ready to shoot myself, but then when I came here it was like being with family."

Well, I'll be darned, Sterling thought. That's Chet Armstrong, the sportscaster. He was just starting out on Channel 11 when I got beaned. He was a skinny kid then, but the way he delivered the sports news, you'd think every play was crucial. Now he's broad shouldered, white haired, and has the craggy face of a man who spent a great deal of time outdoors.

"I felt almost guilty that Christmas Day turned out to be so pleasant," Armstrong continued, "but I knew Peggy was probably smiling down on me."

I wonder if Peggy ever did time in the celestial waiting room, Sterling thought. He wished Chet would open his wallet. Maybe he was carrying her picture.

"Peggy was a terrific gal," Dennis, a beefy redhead with large, agile hands, agreed as he polished beer glasses and filled orders from the slips of paper the waiters dropped in front of him. Sterling noticed that Armstrong's eyes darted to one of the framed pictures over the bar. He leaned forward to get a good look at it. It was a picture of Nor with Chet, whose arm was around the shoulders of a petite woman who had to be Peggy.

I *did* see her, Sterling thought. She was a couple of rows behind me in the waiting room. But she didn't stay there long enough to really settle in.

"Peggy was a lot of fun, but don't get on her bad side," Chet reminisced with a chuckle.

Oh, that's what delayed her, Sterling thought. She had a bit of a temper.

"Listen," Dennis said in the tone of a father confessor, "I know it seems impossible, but I bet that someday down the line you'll meet someone. You've still got plenty of time."

Just watch who you play golf with, Sterling reflected.

"Turned seventy last March, Dennis."

"Today that's young."

Sterling shook his head. I'd be ninety-six. No one would accuse me of being a spring chicken.

"How long have you been here anyhow, Dennis?" Chet asked.

Thank you, Chet, Sterling thought, hoping that Dennis's reply would be a big help in his getting the lay of the land.

"Nor opened this place twenty-three years ago. Bill died just when Billy was starting school. She didn't want to be on the road anymore. I knew her from one of the clubs in New York. After six months, she gave me a call. She'd caught her bartender with his hand in the till. Our kids were almost school age, and my wife wanted to get out of the city. I've been here ever since."

Out of the corner of his eye, Sterling saw that Billy and Nor were on the way out. I'm falling down on the job, he thought, hurrying to catch up with them as they walked across the parking lot.

He was not surprised to see that they had one of those little trucks. Must be the style these days. He smiled at the thought of Marissa getting into Roy's staid vehicle. Like any kid, she probably hated her friends to see her associated with anything boring.

He hoisted himself into the backseat as Billy was turning the key in the ignition, then glanced over his shoulder at the boxes of what appeared to be musical equipment. If only they knew they had a "groupie" in the backseat, Sterling chuckled to himself.

Settled in, he stretched his legs. I don't miss being crowded by baby seats, he thought. He realized he was looking forward to the party. At the party the night before his final golf game, they had been playing Buddy Holly and Doris Day records. It would be fun if Nor and Billy sang like them, he mused.

The car drove through the snow-covered streets of Madison Village. Reminds me of Currier and Ives, Sterling thought, looking at the well-kept houses, many of them tastefully adorned with holiday lights. Evergreen wreaths with holly berries graced front doors. Festive Christmas trees sparkled through parlor windows.

On one lawn, the sight of a beautiful crèche with exquisitely carved figures provoked a wistful smile.

Then they passed a house with a dozen lifesized plastic angels cavorting on the lawn. That bossy angel at the door of the Heavenly Council room should get a load of that monstrosity, he thought.

He caught a glimpse of Long Island Sound. I always liked the North Shore of the Island, he reflected, as he craned his neck for a better look at the water, but it's a lot more built up than it used to be.

In the front seat, Nor and Billy were chuckling about Marissa's attempts to be with them so she could see for herself the inside of the big house.

"She's some piece of goods," Billy said proudly. "She takes after you, Mom. Always with her ear to the ground, afraid she'll miss something."

Agreeing, Nor laughed. "I prefer to call it a healthy interest in her surroundings. Shows how smart she is."

As Sterling listened, his spirits fell. He knew that their lives were about to change and that they were soon to be separated from this child who was the center of their lives.

He only wished he had the power to prevent it.

Whenever Junior and Eddie Badgett held an event in their mansion, Junior had an attack of nerves. Here we go, Charlie Santoli thought as he followed the baseball bat and the bowling ball brothers. Junior, the baseball bat, had small, cold eyes. Eddie, the bowling ball, was always in tears when he talked about Mama, hard as nails about everything else.

The usual flurry of activity before a party was going on. The florists were scurrying around, placing holiday arrangements throughout the house. The caterer's team was setting up the buffet. Jewel, Junior's airheaded twenty-two-year-old girlfriend, was tripping back and forth in stiletto heels, getting in everyone's way. Junior and Eddie's special confidential assistants, uneasy in jackets and ties, were standing together, looking like the thugs they were.

Before he left home, Charlie had been forced to listen to yet another sermon from his wife about the Badgett brothers.

"Charlie, those two are crooks," she told him. Everybody knows it. You should tell them you don't want to be their lawyer anymore. So what if they put a wing on the senior citizens home? It wasn't their money that did it. Listen, I told you not to get involved with them fifteen years ago. Did you listen? No. You'll be lucky if you don't end up in the trunk of a car, and I don't mean a rumble seat. Quit. You've got enough money. You're sixty-two years old, and you're so nervous you twitch in your sleep. I want the grandchildren to know you in the flesh and not have to kiss your picture good night."

It was no use trying to explain to Marge that he couldn't get out. He had intended to handle only the various legitimate businesses of the Badgett brothers. To his regret, however, he had learned that when you lie down with dogs, you get up with fleas, and a number of times he'd been coerced into suggesting to potential government witnesses that it would be worth their while financially—and physically—to forget about certain events. In that way he had managed to prevent the brothers from being indicted for a number of criminal activities, including loan-sharking, fixing basketball games, and illegal bookmaking. So to refuse to do anything they requested of him, or to try to quit working for them, was tantamount to committing suicide.

Today, because of the magnitude of their donation to the senior citizens center, a two million dollar wing given in honor of their mother, they'd managed to get an A-list of guests to come to celebrate their absent mother's eighty-fifth birthday. Both U.S. Senators from New York, the Commissioner of Health and Human Services, various mayors and dignitaries, and the entire board of governors of the senior citizens center would be there. The board alone included some of the most prominent names on Long Island.

In all, a total of about seventy-five people would be present, the kind of people who would give the brothers the aura of respectability they craved.

It was essential that the party go well.

The main event would be held in the grand salon, a room that combined various aspects of a French royal palace. Bright gold walls, spindly gilt chairs, ornate rosewood tables, satin draperies, tapestries, and hovering over all, the reproduction of a two-story-high fifteenth-century marble fireplace, replete with sculpted cherubs, unicorns, and pineapples. Junior had explained that pineapples "symbolized lots of good luck," and he'd instructed the decorator to make sure there were lots of pineapples on the reproduction and to forget about some of those other doohickeys.

The result was a room that was a monument to bad taste, Charlie thought, and he could only imagine the reaction of the social set.

The party was scheduled to begin at five and last until eight. Cocktails, hors d'oeuvres, and a sumptuous buffet would be served. The entertainment would be provided by Billy Campbell, the up-and-coming rock singer, and his mother, Nor Kelly, the former cabaret singer. They were very popular throughout the North Shore. The highlight of the evening would occur at 7:30 P.M. when, via satellite hookup from Wallonia, the mother of the Badgett brothers would be present to hear the assemblage sing "Happy Birthday Heddy-Anna."

"You sure you got enough food?" Junior was asking the caterer.

"Relax, Mr. Badgett, you've ordered enough food to feed an army." Conrad Vogel, the caterer, smiled dismissively.

"I didn't ask you to feed an army. I wanna know if you've got enough fancy food so that if somebody likes one thing and eats a ton of it, you won't be telling him there's none left."

Charlie Santoli watched as the caterer withered under Junior's icy glare. You don't dis Junior, pal, he thought.

The caterer got the message. "Mr. Badgett, I assure you that the food is extraordinary and your guests will be very pleased."

"They better be."

"How about Mama's cake?" Eddie asked. "It better be perfect."

A tiny bead of perspiration was forming over Conrad Vogel's upper lip. "It was specially made by the finest bakery in New York. Their cakes are so good that one of our most demanding clients used them for all four of her weddings. The pastry chef himself is here, just in case the cake requires any slight touch-up after it's unboxed."

Junior brushed past the caterer and went to study Mama Heddy-Anna's portrait, which would be formally presented to the senior center's trustees to be hung in the reception area of the center's new wing. It had been painted by a Wallonian artist and ornately framed by a New York gallery. Junior's phoned instructions to the artist had been precise: "Show Mama to be the beautiful lady she is."

Charlie had seen snapshots of Mama. The portrait of a

handsome matriarch in black velvet and pearls bore not the slightest resemblance to any of them, thank God. The artist had been handsomely rewarded for his services.

"She looks real nice," Junior conceded. Immediately his moment of satisfaction evaporated. "Where are those people I'm paying to sing? They're supposed to be here by now."

Jewel had come up behind him. Slipping an arm through his, she said, "I just saw them turn in to the driveway, sweetie pie. Don't worry about them. They're good, really good."

"They better be. You recommended them."

"You heard them sing, lovey. Remember I took you to Nor's Place for dinner?"

"Yeah, I forgot. They're okay. Good restaurant, good food. Good location. Wouldn't mind owning it myself. Let's take a look at the cake."

With Jewel still on his arm, her flaming red hair dancing around her shoulders, her microminiskirt barely reaching her thighs, Junior led the inspection tour into the kitchen. The pastry chef, his towering white hat regally settled on his head, was standing beside the five-layered birthday cake.

As he saw them approach, he beamed with pride. "Is it not magnificent?" he asked, kissing his fingertips. "A spun-sugar masterpiece. My finest, finest effort. A worthy tribute to your beloved mother. And the taste. The divine taste. Your guests will cherish every bite."

Junior and Eddie walked reverently to view the masterpiece. Then, as one, they began shouting.

"Stupid!"

"Jerk!"

"Dope!"

"It's HEDDY-ANNA, not BETTY-ANNA," Eddie snarled. "My mama's name is *Heddy*-Anna!"

The pastry chef looked incredulous as he wrinkled his nose and frowned. "*Heddy*-Anna???"

"Don't you dare make fun of my mama's name!" Eddie shouted as his eyes welled with tears.

Don't let anything else go wrong, Charlie Santoli prayed. They'll both lose it if anything else goes wrong.

It was a supreme effort for Hans Kramer even to begin the fifteen-minute drive from his home in Syosset to the Badgett brothers' mansion on Long Island Sound. Why did I ever borrow from them? he asked himself for the thousandth time as he turned onto the Long Island Expressway. Why didn't I just declare bankruptcy and have done with it?

An electronics executive, forty-six-year-old Hans had quit his job two years earlier, taken his retirement fund and all his savings and mortgaged his home to open a dot-com company to sell software he had designed. After a promising start, with orders rushing in and the warehouse filled with inventory, the technology industry had crashed. Then the cancellations began. In desperate need of immediate cash, and in an effort to keep the business afloat, he had borrowed from the Badgett brothers. Unfortunately, his efforts so far hadn't paid off.

There's no way on God's earth I can raise the two hundred thousand dollars I borrowed from them, not to mention the fifty percent interest they've added, he despaired.

I must have been out of my mind to go near them. But I've

got a great line of products, he reasoned. If I can just hang in there, things will turn around. Only now I've got to convince the Badgetts to let me renew the note.

In the year since his financial troubles began, Hans had lost twenty pounds. His light brown hair had become streaked with gray. He knew his wife, Lee, was worried sick about him, although she had no idea how bad the situation was. He hadn't told her about the loan, opting instead to tell her only that they needed to cut back on their spending. Why, they'd even practically given up going out for dinner.

The next exit off the expressway led to the Badgett mansion. Hans felt his palms begin to sweat. I was so cocky, he thought as he flicked on the turn signal. Came over here from Switzerland when I was twelve years old and didn't speak a word of English. Graduated from M.I.T. with high honors and thought I'd set the world on fire. And I did for a while. I thought I was immune to failure.

Five minutes later he was approaching the Badgett estate. The gates were open. Cars were lined up, waiting to be admitted by a guard at the foot of the long and winding driveway. Obviously the Badgetts were having a party.

Hans was both relieved and disappointed. I'll phone and leave a message, he thought. Maybe, just maybe, they'll give me an extension.

As he made a U-turn, he tried to ignore the voice inside him that warned that people like the Badgetts never give extensions.

Sterling, Nor, and Billy entered the rear door of the Badgett mansion just in time to hear the insults being heaped on the hapless pastry chef. Sterling hastened into the kitchen to see what was going on and found the chef frantically adjusting something in the lettering on the cake.

Wrong age? Sterling wondered. He'd been at a party once where the twelve-year-old daughter had baked a birthday cake as a surprise for her mother. When she proudly carried out the cake, candles blazing, the mother had nearly fainted. The age she had so carefully concealed was starkly revealed in hot-pink lettering on the vanilla cake. I remember thinking that anyone who couldn't read could always count, Sterling thought. That wasn't too charitable of me.

Fortunately this chef's mistake was small. With a few twirls of his pastry tube, he changed Betty-Anna to Heddy-Anna. Nor and Billy had been drawn to the kitchen by the uproar. "Just make sure not to sing 'Happy Birthday, Betty-Anna,' " Nor whispered to Billy.

"I'm tempted, but I want to get out of here alive."

Sterling tagged along as they went into the salon. Nor ran her fingers over the piano; Billy took his guitar out of the case, and they tested the microphones and sound system.

Charlie Santoli had the responsibility of giving them a list of songs that were favorites of the brothers. "They don't want you blasting your music so loud that people can't think," he said nervously.

"We're musicians. We don't blast," Nor snapped.

"But when Mama is hooked up via satellite, you'll be leading the 'Happy Birthday' song, and then they want you to really project."

The bell rang and the first wave of guests were admitted.

Sterling had always liked being around people. He studied the guests as they came in, and as he listened, realized that there were some pretty important people present.

His general impression was that they were here purely because of the largesse of the donation to the senior citizens center, and that after the party they would be happy to forget the Badgett brothers. But a number of the guests stopped to admire the portrait that would be hanging in the new wing.

"Your mother is a beautiful woman," the president of the center's board of governors said sincerely, nodding at the portrait. "So elegant, so dignified. Does she come to visit you often?"

"My precious mother isn't a good traveler," Junior told her.

"Mama gets airsick and seasick," Eddie mourned.

"Then of course you visit her in Wallonia," she suggested.

Charlie Santoli had joined them. "Of course they do, as frequently as possible," he said smoothly.

Sterling shook his head. He's not telling the truth.

Billy and Nor started their first song and were immediately surrounded by an appreciative audience. Nor was a fine musician with an attractive, husky voice. Billy, however, was exceptional. Standing in the crowd, Sterling listened to the murmured comments.

"He's a young Billy Joel . . ."

"He's going to be a star . . ."

"And he's gorgeous," the daughter of one of the board members cooed.

"Billy, let's hear 'Be There When I Awake.' "

The request brought spontaneous applause.

His fingers moving lightly on the strings of the guitar, Billy began to sing, "I know what I want . . . I know what I need."

That must be his hit record, Sterling thought. Even to my out-of-date ears, it's great.

Thanks to the music, the atmosphere at the party loosened up. The guests began interacting, allowing their glasses to be refilled with the excellent wines, and piling their plates with the truly spectacular food.

By 7:15 the Badgett brothers were beaming. Their party was a success. They were a success.

At that point, Junior picked up the microphone and cleared his throat. "I wanna welcome all of you, and my brother and me hope you're enjoying yourselves very much. It is our pleasure to have you as our guests, and we are very, very happy to have given you the money, I mean donated the money, for the wing of the senior citizens center to be known as the Mama Heddy-Anna wing in honor of our saintly mother's eighty-fifth birthday. And now, by the miracle of satellite, from the historic village of Kizkek where my brother and me were raised, our mama will appear. Mama stayed up way past her bedtime to be with us 'cause she's so honored. Now I ask all of you to join in singing 'Happy Birthday' to her. Our wonderful Billy Campbell and his mother, that doll Nor Kelly, will lead us in song."

There was a faint smattering of applause. The birthday cake was rolled out, ablaze with eighty-six candles, one to grow on. The ten-foot screen dropped down from the ceiling, and Mama Heddy-Anna's dour face emerged to fill it.

She was seated in her rocking chair, sipping grappa.

Eddie's eyes streamed with tears, and Junior blew kisses at the screen as the guests dutifully sang "Happy Birthday, Heddy-Anna" in Wallonian, working from phonetically marked song sheets.

Her cheeks puffed like twin red balloons, Mama blew out the candles on the cake her sons had sent by chartered plane to Wallonia. That was when it became all too clear that she'd filled the hours past her usual bedtime by drinking more than her share of grappa. In broken English she started cursing and complaining loudly that her sons never came to see her and she wasn't feeling so hot.

Junior quickly turned down the volume but not before she had screamed, "How much bad things you two do, you can't come see your mama before she die? Not once you come in all these years."

Billy and Nor immediately started another vigorous round of "Happy Birthday, Heddy-Anna." This time no one joined in, however, and the telecast closed on the unforgettable sight of Mama thumbing her nose at her offspring and their guests, as she came down with a case of the hiccups.

Jewel's laugh was a high-pitched trill. "Doesn't Mama have a wonderful sense of humor? I just love her."

Junior brushed Jewel aside and stalked out of the room. Eddie followed close behind.

Nor quickly whispered to Billy, "This is a disaster. What should we do? He told us to sing 'For She's a Jolly Good Fellow' while people ate the cake.

"And then the medley of songs about mothers, starting with 'I always loved my mama, she's my favorite girl . . .' "

How about "Little old lady, time for tea," Sterling thought. That was a hit in my day.

"We'd better check on what they want us to do now. I'm not taking any chances on second-guessing them," Nor said, glancing around the room at the stunned expressions on the faces of the guests.

As Sterling trotted after Nor and Billy, he sensed imminent disaster. Junior and Eddie were disappearing into a room at the end of the hall.

Billy and Nor raced to catch up with them, and Billy tapped on the now-closed door. When there was no response, he and Nor looked at each other. "Let's take a chance," Nor whispered.

Just go home, Sterling urged, but knew it was a year too late to even think that.

Billy turned the handle and cautiously opened the door. He and Nor stepped into what appeared to be a small reception room. It was empty.

"They're in there," Nor whispered, pointing to an inner room that could be seen through a partially open door. "Maybe we'd better . . ."

"Wait a minute. They're checking the answering machine."

An electronic voice was announcing, "You have one new message."

Nor and Billy hesitated, not sure whether to wait or to leave, but then the message they were overhearing froze them to the spot.

It was a plea from a man who sounded desperate, begging for "wery little extra time" to pay back a loan.

The answering machine clicked off, and they heard Junior shout, "Your time just ran out, buddy. Eddie, get on it. Tell the guys to burn his stinking warehouse down and do it now. I don't wanna hear that it's still standing tomorrow."

"There won't be nuthin' left," Eddie assured him, sounding much cheerier, his mind off Mama for the moment.

Billy put his finger to his lips. Silently he and Nor tiptoed from the room and hurried back to the salon. "Let's get our stuff," Billy whispered. "We're out of here."

What they did not notice, but Sterling did, was that Charlie Santoli, at the other end of the hall, had seen them come out of the office.

The celestial waiting room was filled with newcomers gazing around and trying to adjust to their surroundings. The angel in charge had been ordered to hang a large DO NOT DISTURB sign on the door of the conference room. There had been several instances of former top executives, not used to being kept waiting, who had rushed in demanding a meeting when the angel's back was turned.

Inside the conference room, the Heavenly Council was following Sterling's activities with keen interest.

"Did you notice how chagrined he was when Marissa didn't even sense that he was present in the restaurant?" the nun asked. "He was truly taken aback."

"That was one of the first lessons we wanted him to learn," the monk stated. "During his lifetime, too many people were invisible to him. He'd look right past them."

"Do you think Mama Heddy-Anna will turn up in our waiting room soon?" the shepherd asked. "She told her sons she's dying."

The nurse smiled. "She used the oldest trick in the book to get her sons to visit her. She's as strong as a bull."

"I wouldn't want her in the ring with me," the matador commented wryly.

"That lawyer is in real trouble," said the saint who had reminded Sterling of Pocahontas. "Unless he does something drastic very soon, when his time comes, he won't be dealing with us."

"Poor Hans Kramer is desperate," the nun observed. "The Badgett brothers have absolutely no mercy."

"They belong in the brig," the admiral proclaimed sternly.

"Did you hear that?" the queen's tone was shocked. "They're going to set that poor man's warehouse on fire."

Shaking their heads, the saints fell silent, reflecting sadly on man's inhumanity to man.

Valets frantically rushed to deliver the cars of the guests pouring out of the house. Sterling leaned against a column on the porch, bent on hearing the reactions of the departing merrymakers.

"Bizarre!"

"Give them their money back. *I'll* donate two million for that wing," a dowager snapped.

"Reminded me of the movie 'Throw Momma From the Train.' I bet that's what those two characters feel like doing now," a board member's husband snickered.

"At least the food was good," someone said charitably.

"I hope you caught that they haven't set foot in Wallonia since they left. Figure out why."

"You got a load of Mama, didn't you?"

Sterling noticed that the two U.S. Senators were screaming at their top aides as they were whisked away. They're probably worrying that they'll be written up in the tabloids for partying with mobsters, Sterling thought. They should know what Junior is going to do to some poor guy's warehouse. He couldn't wait to slip into Nor and Billy's car and hear what they had to say about everything that had happened.

A guest, who clearly had slurped as much vodka as Mama had grappa began to sing, "Happy Birthday, Heddy-Anna" in Wallonian, but didn't have his phonetically marked song sheet to consult. He switched to English and was joined by several other guests, who were also feeling no pain.

Sterling heard a valet ask one of the guests if his vehicle was an SUV. What's that? Sterling wondered. A moment later the valet pulled up in one of those little trucks. So that's what it is, Sterling thought. I wonder what SUV stands for.

Billy's SUV was parked in the back. Don't want to miss them, Sterling thought. Two minutes later, when Nor and Billy appeared, lugging their equipment, he was in the backseat.

It was obvious from the nervous expressions on both their faces that they were deeply worried.

Wordlessly, they loaded the car, jumped in, and joined the line of vehicles exiting the long driveway. They did not speak until they were out on the main road. Then Nor asked, the words rushing out, "Billy, do you think they were serious about burning down someone's warehouse?"

"Absolutely, and we're damn lucky they don't know we overheard them."

Uh-oh, Sterling thought. Their lawyer—what's his name? Charlie Santoli—saw you come out of the office. If he tells the Badgetts, your goose is cooked.

"I can't help thinking that I've heard that voice before, the one on the phone message," Nor said slowly. "Did you notice he said 'wery,' not 'very,' when he asked for more time?"

"Now that you say it, I guess I did," Billy agreed. "I just figured the poor guy was so nervous he was practically stuttering."

"No, it wasn't that. Maybe he has a slight lisp. I think he's had dinner at the restaurant. The thing is, if I could only remember who it was, then we could warn him."

"When we get to the restaurant, I'm going to call the police," Billy said. "I don't want to use the cell phone."

They rode the rest of the way in silence. In the backseat, Sterling shared their anxiety.

It was nearly nine o'clock when they entered Nor's Place. The holiday diners were in full force. Nor tried to greet people quickly. At the same moment, she and Billy spotted one of their old friends, Sean O'Brien, a retired detective, sitting at the bar.

They looked at each other. "I'll ask him to sit with us. He'll know what we should do," Billy said.

A smile plastered on her face, Nor went to her usual table at the front of the restaurant. From this vantage point she could oversee the operation, hold court, and easily greet her patrons. Sterling joined her, taking the seat he'd been occupying a few hours earlier.

Billy came to the table followed by Sean O'Brien, a solid-looking man of about fifty-five, with a full head of graying brown hair, alert brown eyes, and a genial smile.

"Season's greetings, Nor," he began, then immediately sensed something was wrong. "What's up?" he asked abruptly, as he and Billy sat down.

"We were hired for a party the Badgett brothers gave this afternoon," Nor began.

"The Badgett brothers?" O'Brien raised one eyebrow, then listened intently as they told him of the message on the answering machine and Junior Badgett's response to it.

"I know the voice," Nor finished. "I'm sure that man has been a customer here."

"Nor, the feds have been trying to pin something on those two for years. They're as slippery as fish in olive oil. They're crooks and they're vicious. If that was a local call, I wouldn't be surprised to be reading tomorrow about a warehouse that burned down overnight."

"Is there anything we can do to try to stop them?" Billy asked.

"I can alert the feds, but those guys have interests all over. We know for sure they have a presence in Vegas and Los Angeles. That message could have come from anywhere, but no matter where it came from, it doesn't mean the warehouse is in that vicinity."

"I never knew the Badgetts were that bad," Billy said. "You hear rumors, but they have those car and boat dealerships . . ."

"They've got a dozen legitimate businesses," O'Brien said.

"That's the way they launder their money. I'll make some calls. The feds will at least want to keep them under surveillance, but those guys never dirty their own hands."

Nor rubbed her forehead, her face troubled. "There's a reason I remember that voice. Wait a minute." She beckoned a waiter. "Sam, ask Dennis to join us. You cover the bar."

O'Brien looked at her. "It's better if nobody else knows you overheard that conversation."

"I trust Dennis with my life," Nor said.

The table is getting crowded, Sterling thought. I'll have to stand. He felt the chair being pulled out and jumped up quickly. He had no desire to have Dennis sitting on his lap.

" . . . and, Dennis, I'm sure I've heard that voice in this restaurant," Nor concluded a few minutes later. "He pronounced 'very' as 'wery.' Granted that could have been just nerves, but I thought maybe it's a guy who sits at the bar and talks with you sometimes."

Dennis shook his head. "I can't think of a soul, Nor. But I do know this—if that Badgett guy was on the level when he talked about burning down a warehouse, the fellow who called him will be 'wery upset.' "

"Wery, wery upset," Billy agreed.

They all laughed nervously.

They're trying to use humor to cover their very real anxieties, Sterling thought. If the Badgett brothers are as bad as Sean O'Brien believes they are, and if Nor and Billy have to testify about that call . . . Poor Marissa. She was so happy today.

O'Brien got up. "I've got to make some phone calls," he said. "Nor, can I use your office?"

"Of course."

"You and Billy come with me. I want to put you on the phone and have you repeat exactly what you heard."

"I'll be at the bar." Dennis pushed his chair back.

If I were still alive, that chair would have smashed my big toe, Sterling thought.

"Nor, I thought you and Billy were doing a holiday performance here at the restaurant tonight," a patron at a nearby table called. "We came specially to hear you two sing."

"You're going to." Nor smiled. "We'll be back in fifteen minutes."

In the office, O'Brien phoned his contact at the FBI, and Nor and Billy recounted what they had overheard. When the call ended, Nor shrugged her shoulders. "It is what it is. Unless I can remember whose voice that is, I'm no use to them."

Billy's cell phone rang. "It's Rissa," he said as he looked at the Caller ID. His troubled expression cleared. "Hi, baby . . . We just got back . . . No, we didn't see the swimming pool or the bowling alley . . . Well, I wouldn't say they were like the Sopranos."

"I would," Nor murmured.

"Uh-huh, we did our usual bit . . ." He laughed. ". . . Of course we were sensational. They couldn't get enough of us.

Listen, baby, NorNor will say a quick hello, then you get to bed. I'll see you tomorrow. Love you."

He handed the phone to Nor, then turned to O'Brien. "You've met my daughter, Marissa, haven't you?"

"Sure. I thought she owned this place."

"She thinks she does."

Nor said good night to Marissa and smiled ruefully as she snapped the phone closed and handed it to Billy. She looked at O'Brien. "I can't help wondering if that poor guy who was begging for more time to pay off a loan is supporting a family."

Billy put his arm around her shoulders and gave her a quick hug. "You look tired, Mom, so I hate to say it, but your public awaits . . ."

"I know. We've got to get out there. Give me a minute to do my face."

O'Brien reached in his pocket. "Here's my card. If you get a brainstorm, call me at any time. I'll give one to Dennis too."

By 9:30, when Nor and Billy began to perform, every table in the restaurant was filled. They did two half-hour shows, one at 9:30, then another at 11, for the late-night crowd.

They're troupers, Sterling thought. You'd never know they have a care in the world. The minute Nor finished the first show she slipped into her office, carrying the reservations books for the last two years under her arm. Sterling sat with her as she went through them, saying each name aloud as she went down the list.

Several times she stopped and repeated a name, then shook her head and continued to read. She's trying to see if the name of the guy whose voice they heard jumps out at her, Sterling thought.

The concern in Nor's face deepened as she spoke name after name. But then she glanced at her watch and jumped up, opened her bag and pulled out her compact. In seconds she had lightly powdered her face, touched up her eyes and lips. She pulled the jeweled comb out of her hair and shook her head. Sterling was amazed at how deftly she twisted the long tresses in her fingers, swept them up, and anchored them once again.

"I feel like Minnie off the pickle boat," she said aloud, "but I guess the show must go on."

You look wonderful, Sterling wanted to protest. You're a really beautiful woman. And who the heck is Minnie off the pickle boat?

At the door of the office, Nor let out a quick sigh, but a moment later she was wreathed in smiles as she stopped at table after table to exchange a few words with her patrons.

This place is full, Sterling noticed, and it's obvious from the way Nor talks to everyone that they're all regulars. They seem so glad to have a word with her. Well, she's good. He listened as she inquired about someone's mother, someone's son, another's planned vacation, then congratulated a couple who had just become engaged.

The Heavenly Council will never tell her that she didn't pay attention to other people, Sterling thought. That's for sure. Too bad I wasn't more like her.

Billy was deep in conversation with a man and woman at a corner table. Sterling decided to tune in. I hope nobody else joins us, he thought as he took the one empty chair. Then as he caught the gist of the conversation, he raised his eyebrows. These people were executives from Empire Recording Company, and they wanted to sign Billy to a contract.

The man was saying, "I don't have to tell you the kind of people we've launched. We've been scouting you for a while, and you've got it, Billy. We're offering you a two-album contract."

"I'm very flattered and it sounds great, but you'll have to talk to my agent," Billy said, smiling.

He's trying to hide that he's thrilled, Sterling realized. It's every young singer's dream to be signed up by a record company. What a crazy day.

The last stragglers left the restaurant at 12:30. Nor and Billy sat at the bar with Dennis as he finished cleaning up. Nor held up a glass. "I've heard it's bad luck to toast with water, but I'm going to take a chance. Here's to Billy and the new contract."

"Your dad would be so proud," Dennis said.

"You bet he would." Nor looked up. "Here's to you, Bill, wherever you are up there. Your kid's done good."

I definitely have to meet him, Sterling told himself. He saw the suspicious touch of moisture in the eyes of all three.

Billy was just about the age Marissa is now when he lost his dad. It must have been awfully tough on him and Nor.

"Let's keep our fingers crossed that it all goes through," Billy told them. "I don't want to get too excited yet. That'll wait until I have the offer in writing."

"You will," Nor assured him. "But you're still singing with me here at Christmastime next year."

"I know, Mom, and for free," Billy laughed.

"You'll have to hire a bouncer for crowd control," Dennis declared. He folded a towel. "Okay, that's it. Nor, you look awfully tired. Let me drive you home."

"Listen, if I lived fifteen minutes away, the way I feel now, I'd take you up on it. But for the three minutes it'll take me to get there, I'd rather have the car at the door in the morning. You can carry those reservations books out for me. I'm going to keep at them for a while."

She kissed Billy lightly on the cheek. "See you tomorrow."

"Okay. I'm heading upstairs. Don't try to go over those books tonight, Mom. Leave it for the morning."

They looked at each other. "I know," Billy said. "By then it may be too late."

So that's where Billy lives, Sterling thought. He must have an apartment up there. It would be interesting to see what Nor's home is like. She said it's only a three-minute drive away. That can't be too far for me to walk back. Once again he found himself hurrying across the parking lot, this time following Nor and Dennis.

The temperature has really dropped in these few hours, he

thought. He looked up. Clouds were forming and beginning to obscure the moon and stars. He sniffed. There was a hint of snow in the air. I was one of those people who preferred winter to summer, he thought. Annie thought I was crazy. If there was anything she loved, it was a day at the seashore. I remember her family had a place in Spring Lake.

Nor's car was a handsome Mercedes sedan. I used to drive one of these, Sterling thought, and in a lot of ways this one doesn't look that much different from the one I had. As Dennis laid the reservations books on the floor in the back and held the driver's door open for Nor, Sterling got in the front seat. I never liked to ride in the back of the car, he thought. My legs always felt cramped.

Nor locked the door and fastened her seat belt. Everybody does that these days, Sterling mused. I wonder if there's a law about it.

He readjusted his homburg, smiling as he remembered that next year Marissa would poke fun at it.

As they pulled out of the driveway, he jumped when Nor muttered aloud, "Mama Heddy-Anna. God help us!"

Sterling felt a little guilty. Nor thinks she's alone, and she's one of those people who talks to herself. I used to do that too, and I'd have died if I learned that someone was eavesdropping on me.

But it's okay because I'm here to help them, he comforted himself. Fortunately she turned on the radio and listened to the news the rest of the way.

Nor's house was at the end of a cul-de-sac, situated on a generous piece of property. The minute he saw it he sensed that it was the perfect home for her. It looked to him like a renovated farmhouse. The exterior was white clapboard with black shutters. The porch light was on, casting a warm glow around the front door.

"Thank God to be home," Nor sighed.

I know what you mean, Sterling said aloud, then rolled his eyes. Thank God she can't hear me. I might have given her a heart attack.

I'm not going to stay long, he promised himself as Nor fished through her purse for her house key, got out of the car, and gathered the reservations books in her arms.

Sterling walked to the front door, admiring the attractive shrubbery that was lightly coated with snow.

As soon as Nor opened the door, shut off the alarm, and switched on the light, he realized that she also had great taste. The ground floor was a single, very large room with white walls and wooden floors. A raised-hearth fireplace defined the living room area. At a right angle to it stood a floor to-ceiling-Christmas tree, decorated with strings of candle-shaped bulbs. The bottom three tiers clearly bore Marissa's touch. Handmade paper ornaments, a quantity of tinsel, and a dozen candy canes demonstrated her idea of how a Christmas tree should look.

Overstuffed couches, Persian area rugs, fine antique furnishings, and first-class paintings filled the rest of the room. The effect was that of vivid serenity—if there is such a thing, Sterling thought.

"Cup of cocoa," Nor murmured as she kicked off her shoes. She walked to the kitchen area, dropped the reservations books on the table, and opened the refrigerator. Hating to rush, Sterling scurried from painting to painting. These are valuable, he thought. I wish I had a chance to really study them. An English hunting scene particularly intrigued him.

As the attorney for a number of family trusts when he was alive, he'd developed an eye for good art. They used to tell me I could have been an appraiser, he remembered.

A staircase to the second floor beckoned him. One quick look and then I'm off, he promised himself.

Nor's bedroom was the largest. Framed pictures were on the bureau, the dressing table, and the night tables. These were all personal and many of them were of a much younger Nor with Billy's father. There were at least a half-dozen of Billy with his parents, starting from the time he was an infant. He seemed to be about six years old in the last one that showed the three of them together.

Sterling poked his head into the first of the other two bedrooms. It was small but cozy, with the uncluttered look of a guest room.

The third door was closed. The small porcelain tile on it said MARISSA'S PLACE. As he opened the door, Sterling felt a lump in his throat. This child is about to lose out on so much in this upcoming year, he thought.

The room was enchanting. White wicker furniture. Blue-and-white wallpaper. White eyelet bedspread and curtains. Shelves of books on one wall. A desk with a bulletin board against another.

He heard Nor's footsteps on the stairs. It was time to go. Remembering the door had been closed, he quietly pulled it shut, then watched as Nor went into her room. A moment later, with the collar of his chesterfield turned up, his homburg pulled down as far as he could get it, Sterling walked briskly down the road.

I've got several hours to kill, he thought. Billy's probably asleep. Maybe I'll just drop by and look in on Marissa. But where exactly does she live? I never was too good at directions.

Until now there'd been plenty of activity to keep him occupied, but with everyone going to bed, he felt a little lonely as he trudged through the quiet streets.

Should I try to contact the Heavenly Council? he wondered. Or will they decide I can't do the job? And if so, what then?

Suddenly something caught his eye.

What's that?

A piece of paper was fluttering from the sky. It stopped falling when it was directly in front of him. Sterling plucked it out of the air, unfolded it, and walked to the next street lamp to read it.

It was a map of the village. Marissa's home and Nor's Place were clearly indicated. A dotted line started at a point marked "you are here" and gave specific directions—"four blocks east . . . turn left one block, then right"—showing him the way to Marissa's house. A second dotted line illustrated the way from there back to the restaurant.

Sterling looked up, past the moon, past the stars, into eternity. Thank you. I am very grateful, he whispered.

No matter how late the hour, Dennis Madigan always read the *New York Post* before settling down to sleep. His wife, Joan, had long ago learned to sleep with his light on.

Tonight, however, he could not concentrate on the paper. He knew neither Nor nor Billy realized that their lives could be in serious danger. If the Badgetts were as bad as Sean O'Brien portrayed them . . . Dennis shook his head. When he worked in bars in Manhattan, he'd seen and heard a lot about their kind. None of it good.

Very. "Wery." What is this reminding me of? he asked himself as he irritably flipped through the pages of the newspaper. Nor thinks the man might be someone who comes into the restaurant. He can't be a regular, though, or I'd know him.

"Wery," he said aloud.

Joan opened her eyes and blinked. "What?"

"Nothing. Sorry, honey. Go back to sleep."

"Easy for you to say," she muttered as she turned her back to him.

Dennis skipped to the *Post*'s television section and smiled as he read Linda Stasi's funny review of a corny holiday special.

Still not remotely sleepy even though it was 3:30, he began to skim the restaurant pages. The write-up on a new midtown restaurant caught his eye. "We started with vichyssoise . . . ," the columnist began.

Sounds like a good joint, Dennis thought. Have to check it out. He and Joan enjoyed going into the city occasionally and trying new places.

He stared at the paper. Vichyssoise. He remembered a smart aleck waiter at Nor's—one who didn't last long—joking that a customer who ordered "wichyssoise" last time, now would like a cup of "wegetable" soup.

What's the customer's name? Dennis thought. I can see him. He and his wife always had a cocktail at the bar. Nice people. I didn't think of him right away because that's the only hint of an accent he had, and he hasn't been around in a long time . . .

In his mind, he could see a face. He's local, Dennis thought. And his name . . . his name . . . it sounds European . . .

Hans Kramer!

That's it! That's his name!

Dennis grabbed the phone. Nor answered on the first ring. "Nor, I've got it. The guy on the answering machine. Could it be Hans Kramer?"

"Hans Kramer," she said, slowly. "That doesn't ring a bell with me. I don't remember . . ."

"Think, Nor. He ordered 'wichyssoise' and 'wegetable' soup."

"Oh my God, of course . . . you're right." Nor leaned on one elbow and pulled herself up. Sean O'Brien's card was propped against the lamp on her night table. As she reached for it she could feel adrenaline surging through her body.

"I know Kramer has something to do with computers, Dennis. Maybe he has a warehouse. I'll call Sean O'Brien this minute. I just hope we're not too late."

As Sterling approached Marissa's house, everything looked quiet and peaceful. All was dark inside except for a faint light shining through an upstairs window.

My mother used to leave the hall light on for me, he remembered. And she'd leave my bedroom door open a crack so I could see it. I was chicken, he thought with a smile. Never mind the light, I slept with my teddy bear till I was ten.

Noting a small sign that indicated the house was wired against intruders, he slipped inside, not bothering to open the door just in case the alarm was on. He had the feeling that the Heavenly Council wanted him to move around like everybody else except when it prevented him from doing his job, but he was very sure they didn't want him setting off alarms.

He tiptoed up the stairs and stepped over Roy's safety gate, hoisting his leg high to clear it. How big does he think those kids are anyhow? Sterling wondered as he felt a tug on the cuff of his trousers. The next thing he knew he was tumbling onto the hallway floor.

Thank God I don't make any noise, he thought as he stared up at the ceiling. His hat had gone flying. He got up slowly, aware of a faint twinge in his back. Retrieving the homburg, he resumed his attempt to visit Marissa.

Her bedroom was the last one at the end of the hallway. All the bedroom doors were slightly ajar. A light snore was coming from inside the master bedroom. As he passed the munchkins' room, he could hear the sound of one of the boys stirring. Sterling hesitated and listened closely, but then the child seemed to settle down again.

Even though the night was beginning to cloud over, there was enough light from the heavens for him to see Marissa's face clearly. She was curled up in bed, her hair soft on her cheek, the covers tucked around her.

A pile of boxes in the corner were testimony to the fact that she had received an abundance of presents for Christmas and her birthday. Not surprising, Sterling thought. I'd love to be able to give her something myself.

He sat in the same chair he would sit in next year, when he would talk to Marissa for the first time. From there he could study her face. She looks like an angel, he thought tenderly. If only she didn't have to go through the change that is coming. If only I had the power to keep her world the way it is now. But I can't, so next year I'll do everything I can to put her world back together again. By hook or by crook, he resolved.

And not just because I want to go to heaven. I truly want to help her. She looks so small and vulnerable. Hard to believe she's the same kid who was trying to call the shots at the restaurant today, and who didn't waste any time phoning her father to get the lowdown on the party.

With a smile that ended in a sigh, Sterling got up and left the room. As he went down the hallway he heard one of the munchkins start to cry. Then the other one joined in.

Luckily, they don't need me, Sterling thought. An instant later Roy staggered out of the bedroom and into the nursery. "Daddy's here," he crooned. "Roy Junior, Robert, Daddy's here."

Denise has him well trained, Sterling thought. My friends used to turn a deaf ear when their kids started howling in the middle of the night. But times have changed.

I was an only child, he thought as he descended the stairs. My parents were in their forties when I was born. I became the center of their universe. They were in heaven long before I arrived in the celestial waiting room.

It will be so good to see Mother and Dad again, he thought, once more glancing skyward.

Sterling consulted the map before he left the house, then made his way to Nor's restaurant. As he walked through the quiet streets, he suddenly felt an acute sense of urgency. Even though it absolutely was not coming from anyplace nearby, he was beginning to smell smoke.

They did it! he thought. The warehouse fire has just been set.

Sean O'Brien had put in twenty years with the Nassau County Police Department. During that time he had learned to expect predawn phone calls if there was an important development in a case he was working on.

When his phone rang at 3:40, Sean woke up immediately and grabbed it. As he hoped, it was Nor.

"Sean, I just heard from Dennis. He came up with the name of the guy on the answering machine, and he's right. I'm absolutely positive that he's right."

"Who is it?"

"His name is Hans Kramer. He lives in Syosset and has some kind of computer software company. He comes into the restaurant occasionally."

"Okay, Nor. I'll get right on it."

Thoroughly awake now, Sean sat on the side of the bed. He was alone in the room. His wife, Kate, a nurse, was working the night shift on the pediatrics floor of North Shore hospital.

His first call was to police headquarters in Syosset. There was a chance Kramer was known to them.

It proved to be a good bet. Nick Amaretto, the lieutenant

in charge, knew exactly who Kramer was. "Nice guy. He's lived in town twenty years. Was on the zoning board for a while. Ran the Red Cross drive a couple of years ago. Has his own software company."

"Does he have a warehouse?"

"Yeah. He bought property in the area off the expressway that had that string of crummy motels. He built a nice little complex with an office and warehouse."

"I have a tip that it may be torched. A matter of an overdue loan from the Badgett brothers."

"Oh, boy. We'll get over there right away. I'll contact the bomb squad and the fire department."

"I'm calling the feds. Talk to you later."

"Wait a minute, Sean," the lieutenant snapped. "Something big is coming in on the radio."

Sean O'Brien knew even before Amaretto got back on the phone that he was too late. The Kramer complex was already in flames.

Hans Kramer received the call from his security service at 3:43 A.M. The smoke detectors in the warehouse had been activated. The fire department was on the way.

In silent desperation, Hans and his wife, Lee, threw on clothes, stuffed their bare feet into sneakers, grabbed jackets, and ran to the car.

I dropped a lot of the insurance coverage, Hans thought desperately. *I couldn't afford the premiums. If the fire department can't save the warehouse, what will I do?*

He felt a tightening in his chest. Even though the car had not yet warmed up, he was dripping perspiration.

"Hans, you're trembling," Lee said, her voice sick with worry. "No matter how bad it is, we can handle it. I promise, we can handle it."

"Lee, you don't understand. I borrowed money, a lot of money. I thought I could pay it back. I was sure business would pick up." The road was almost empty. He pressed the accelerator and the car raced ahead.

"Hans, the doctor has been warning you. That last stress test you took wasn't good. Please calm down."

I owe them three hundred thousand dollars, Hans thought. The warehouse is worth three million, but I'm only insured enough to cover the mortgage. I won't have enough to pay off the loan.

As they turned onto the street that led to the complex, both Hans and Lee gasped. In the distance they could see flames shooting through the darkness, fierce angry flames surrounded by thick billowing smoke.

"Oh, dear God," Lee breathed.

Hans, in shock, said nothing. *They* did this, Hans thought. The Badgetts. This is their answer to my request for an extension on the loan.

When Hans and Lee reached the warehouse, it was surrounded by fire trucks. Gallons of water from high-powered hoses were pouring into the inferno, but it was obvious the blaze could not be contained.

As Hans pushed open the door of the car, a gigantic wave of pain washed over him, and he toppled onto the driveway.

Moments later he could feel something being clamped over his nostrils, a jolting in his chest, and strong hands lifting him. In a crazy way he felt relieved.

It was all beyond his control.

Sterling arrived back at the restaurant and was not surprised to see Nor getting out of her car in the parking lot. They must know about the fire already, he thought as he broke into a trot.

He followed Nor inside and up to Billy's apartment, which encompassed the entire second floor of the building. Dennis was already there, and Billy had made coffee.

"Sean is on his way over," Nor told Billy. She had no make-up on. Her hair was loosely caught up in a comb, but long tendrils were slipping around her neck and face. She was wearing a light blue sweat suit and a pair of sneakers.

Billy had on rumpled blue jeans, a wrinkled denim shirt, and old moccasins. His eyes looked tired, and he needed a shave.

Dennis was wearing a gray Madison Village sweatshirt over well-worn corduroy pants.

"Sean said it's important that he talk to us right away," Nor said as Billy poured coffee into mugs, and the three of them went to the table in the dining room.

From the chair he selected, Sterling could see into the living room. Billy's place was a comfortable bachelor pad, slightly untidy, with sneakers under the coffee table and a pile of newspapers on top of it. The couch and chairs were basically nondescript but looked inviting.

It was clear that Billy worked on his music in the living room. There were a couple of guitars propped up against the piano, and sheet music was scattered on the couch.

As at Nor's home, many of the homemade ornaments on the Christmas tree looked as though they had Marissa's touch.

The ringing of the doorbell indicated that Sean O'Brien had arrived. Billy buzzed him in and waited as he climbed the stairs.

O'Brien's expression was grave. He nodded when Billy offered coffee, joined them at the table, and told them about the fire.

"How bad is it?" Nor asked.

"About as bad as it gets," O'Brien said. "Hans Kramer is in the hospital. He's had a pretty severe heart attack, but he should make it."

Nor inhaled sharply. "Oh, no."

"His place burned to the ground," O'Brien continued. "There's absolutely nothing left. It was one expert job."

"It was definitely set?" Nor asked flatly, already knowing the answer.

"Yes, it was."

"What happens now?" Billy asked.

"The FBI will be here soon. They need to take statements from you. Your testimony directly implicates the Badgetts.

When Kramer is well enough, we'll get his statement. Then the feds will go for an indictment. Since you overheard Junior's order to torch the warehouse, it looks like this time there will finally be a solid case against them. But I warn you, it's absolutely imperative that no one knows you two are witnesses."

Billy and Nor exchanged glances. "I think we both understand," Billy said.

"I certainly do," Dennis said grimly.

Sterling shook his head. The lawyer, he thought. The Badgetts' lawyer, Charlie Santoli. He saw Billy and Nor coming out of the office. Do the Badgetts know that yet?

On Monday morning at 7:30, Charlie Santoli went downstairs to the kitchen of his home in Little Neck, Long Island. His wife, Marge, was already there preparing breakfast.

Hands on her hips, a worried frown on her face, she took a good look at him. "You look like you've been up for a week, Charlie," she said bluntly.

Charlie raised his hand. "Marge, don't start. I'm okay."

Marge was an attractive, generously sized woman with short brown hair, a shade she preserved by regular visits to the local beauty salon. For years she had kept a standing appointment every Saturday for a wash, set, and manicure. Every fourth Saturday she had a seaweed facial and a color job.

Marge never allowed circumstances to quiet her lively tongue. She had a reputation for conducting conversations with fellow patrons of the salon while sitting under the dryer. Of course this meant that she had to shout to be heard, but, as Charlie had learned, Marge was born with her Irish ancestors' gift of gab. Nothing stood in the way of her having both the first *and* the last word.

Now she continued to scrutinize her husband, studying his face, taking in the lines of fatigue around his eyes, the tightness of his lips, the faint quiver of a muscle in his cheek, and then began a familiar refrain. "You look terrible, and it's all because those two are driving you crazy."

A buzzer went off. Marge turned, and with her mittened hand, removed a tray of freshly baked corn muffins from the oven. "Did you get any sleep at all last night?"

Did I? Charlie wondered. His head was aching, his stomach was knotted and churning. He shrugged his answer.

Yesterday evening, when he arrived home at nine o'clock, Marge had pounced on him for details about the party, but he had begged off. "Marge, give me time to get over it."

Mercifully she had done just that, helped by the fact that a vintage Christmas movie she'd always loved was about to start on an obscure cable station. A box of tissues next to the couch, a cup of tea on the table in front of her, Marge had cheerfully prepared herself for a good cry.

Immensely relieved to have a reprieve, Charlie fixed a strong scotch and buried himself in the Sunday papers.

It had nearly killed Marge to miss the Badgett party, especially with the delicious prospect of seeing Mama Badgett on satellite television. What kept her away was a long-planned, late-afternoon, holiday reunion of her classmates from St. Mary's Academy. As chairperson of the event, she had chosen the date for it and therefore simply could not miss it. As Charlie had pointed out, she was hoist on her own petard.

Now Marge put a muffin on a plate and placed it in front of

him. "Don't stand there," she said. "Sit down and eat like a normal human being."

It was useless to protest. Charlie dutifully pulled out the chair as she poured him a cup of coffee. His vitamins were already lined up next to a glass of freshly squeezed orange juice.

If only he could call up the Badgetts and tell them he wasn't ever going to walk into their home or office again. If only he could just sit here in this cozy kitchen with Marge and have a peaceful breakfast without ever having to think about the brothers again.

Marge poured her own coffee and slathered jam on a muffin. "Now tell me," she ordered. "What happened at the party? The way you dragged yourself in last night, it must have been awful. Didn't the satellite hookup work?"

"Unfortunately, it came through loud and clear."

Her eyes widened. "What do you mean, 'unfortunately?' "

"Mama Heddy-Anna was plastered." Charlie relayed the rest of the story, omitting nothing and finishing with a vivid description of Mama Heddy-Anna thumbing her nose at the North Shore social set.

Frustrated, Marge thumped the table with her clenched fist. "I can't believe I missed that. Why do I only go with you to the boring parties? And to think I was the one who said Thanksgiving weekend was a bad time to have our reunion. What did I ever do to deserve this?"

Charlie sipped the last of his coffee. "I wish I *had* missed it! Those two are going to be in one foul mood today." It was on the tip of his tongue to tell her that it was now obvious to everyone present at the party that the Badgett brothers had not been back to Wallonia since they left it, and to relate to her Mama's own words, "How much bad you do, you can't come visit your mama?"

Charlie had never had the courage to tell Marge that it was only after he was in too deep to get out that he had learned the full extent of the situation in Wallonia. Junior and Eddie had been sentenced, in absentia, to life imprisonment there, for a host of crimes Charlie didn't even want to think about. They could never go back, and he could never get away from them.

With something akin to despair, he got up, kissed the top of Marge's head, went to the closet, put on his overcoat, picked up his briefcase, and left.

The Badgett office building where Charlie worked was in Rosewood, about fifteen minutes away from the estate. Junior and Eddie were already there when Charlie arrived. They were in Junior's private office, and to Charlie's surprise both men were in remarkably good spirits. He had expected them to be in foul moods and to somehow manage to blame at least part of the Mama fiasco on him.

On the drive there from Little Neck he had been preparing his defense: "I suggested you make the donation for the wing, give the party, and present the portrait. The satellite hookup was your idea."

But, of course, Charlie knew that was the last thing he could say. Any hint that Mama's appearance had been less than a delight would be unforgivable. By now the brothers would have figured out another reason why the party had been a colossal flop.

The entertainment, Charlie thought. They'll decide that Nor Kelly and Billy Campbell didn't cut the mustard. They'll blame Jewel for suggesting them and me for hiring them. As he turned into the reserved parking area, he suddenly remembered how upset Kelly and Campbell had been when they came out of Junior's office yesterday.

The brothers must have found fault with the way they sang "Happy Birthday" in Wallonian, Charlie decided. Reluctantly he turned off the ignition, got out of the car, and pressed the "lock" symbol on his key ring. Dragging his feet, he walked to the building and took the elevator to the fourth floor, which was entirely dedicated to the Badgett brothers' quasi-legitimate enterprises.

The reason for the early meeting was that Junior was interested in purchasing a new car dealership in Syosset that was beginning to cut into the profits of his own operation. Junior's secretary was not yet in. As Charlie murmured a greeting to a receptionist and waited to be announced, he wondered how long it would be before the deal closed, before the new dealer got the message that he didn't have a choice not to sell to the Badgetts.

"Tell him to come on in," Junior's genial voice boomed on the intercom.

The office had been done by the same decorator who had lavished his excesses on the mansion. An ornately carved partner desk with a shiny finish, gold-striped wallpaper, a dark brown carpet emblazoned with the brothers' initials in gold, heavy brown satin draperies, and a glass-enclosed miniature village with a plaque inscribed OUR BOYHOOD HOME were only some of the points of interest.

To the left of the door, a couch and chairs upholstered in a zebra pattern were grouped around a forty-inch television screen hung on the wall.

The brothers were drinking coffee and watching the local station. Junior waved Charlie in, pointing to a chair. "The news is coming on, I wanna see it."

"After six hours, the warehouse fire in Syosset is still burning fiercely," the reporter at the news desk began. "Two firemen have been treated for smoke inhalation. The owner of the warehouse, Hans Kramer, suffered a heart attack at the site, and has been removed to St. Francis hospital, where he is now in intensive care . . ."

Vivid images of the blazing building appeared. On a split screen, a tape was rerun of a fireman administering CPR to Hans Kramer, who was stretched on the ground, an oxygen mask clamped over his face.

"That's enough, Eddie. Turn it off." Junior got up. "Still burning, huh? Must be some heck of a fire."

"Faulty wiring, I bet." Eddie shook his head. "Happens, huh, Junior?"

Hans Kramer. Charlie knew that name. He'd been to see

Junior at the mansion. He was one of the people who received "private loans" from the brothers. They did this to him. He didn't pay on time, Charlie thought with absolute certainty, so they burned down his business.

This scenario had been played out before. If the cops can prove Junior and Eddie had anything to do with this fire, they'll be facing another arson charge, Charlie thought, quickly assessing the situation. If Kramer dies, they could be facing a murder rap.

But of course, none of this would ever be traced back to the Badgetts. They were too careful. The loan Kramer signed with them probably had a normal interest rate on the face of the note. No one would know that the fifty percent interest rate had already been built into the principal. And of course the guy who actually set the fire would not be one of the thugs on their payroll. For that they would have contracted a freelancer.

But if anything comes up to tie this fire to Junior and Eddie, I get the job of helping people to forget what they know or think they know, Charlie thought despairingly.

"Hey, Charlie, why so glum?" Junior asked. "It's a beautiful morning."

"Yeah, a really great morning," Eddie echoed, as he got up.

"And, like Jewel said, Mama was cute as a button on the satellite," Junior added. "She always loved her grappa. Like Jewel said, after Eddie and I went into the office yesterday, everyone kept saying that Mama was adorable."

"Yeah," Eddie agreed, his smile becoming nostalgic.

"And those entertainers were something else. Good. I mean really good."

Charlie had not seen Junior bubbling over with such fervent good humor in months. Jewel isn't the airhead I thought she was, he decided. If she managed to convince those two that everybody loved Mama, she ought to be made ambassador to Wallonia.

"I'm glad you liked Nor Kelly and Billy Campbell," he said. "They looked so upset when they came out of your office that I thought maybe you'd told them you weren't satisfied with their music."

Charlie was immediately aware of a drastic change in the atmosphere. Junior looked at him, his eyes cold slits, his cheekbones flushed, the muscles in his neck suddenly prominent. "What did you say?" he asked, his voice chips of ice.

Nervously, Charlie glanced at Eddie, whose bovine cheeks were now rigid. The sweet sentiment evoked by Mama's name had vanished from his eyes. His lips had become a thin, grayish-red gash across his face.

"I simply said that . . ." his voice trailed off . . . "that Nor Kelly and Billy Campbell seemed a little upset when they came out of your office after your mother's satellite visit."

"Why didn't you tell us they were there?"

"Junior, there was no reason. Why would I have told you? I thought you knew."

"Eddie, the door was open from the reception room, wasn't it?" Junior asked.

"Yeah."

"All right, Charlie. You should have told us they followed us in. You should have known it would be important for us to know. Now you're going to have to make a few calls to the songbirds." He paused deliberately. "I think you know what I'm talking about."

I guess that's the end of the questions and the depositions, Sterling thought as he watched the FBI personnel shaking hands with Nor, Billy, Dennis, and Sean. It was now eleven o'clock. For the past two hours, the FBI had been taking sworn statements from the four. They even had Nor and Billy draw a floor plan to show where they were standing when they heard Hans Kramer's voice on the answering machine and Junior's order to burn the warehouse.

"Ms. Kelly, you're sure the Badgetts didn't suspect that you were in the room right outside their office?" Rich Meyers, the head investigator, asked again as he picked up his briefcase. "As I explained, if they knew you overheard them, you'd need to be protected immediately."

"I don't think they knew. From what I understand about the brothers, if they had seen us they probably would have called off their plans for the fire." Nor readjusted the comb that was holding her hair in place. "There's an old expression, 'I feel like something the cat dragged in.' . . .

My mother used to say that, Sterling thought.

". . . and that's exactly the way I feel now. If you're done with me, I'm going to go home, climb in the Jacuzzi, and then get a couple of hours' sleep."

"A very good idea," Meyers said sympathetically. "All right. We'll be in touch with you. In the meantime go about your business as usual."

Sounds easy, Sterling thought. Unfortunately it's not going to work like that.

Sean O'Brien lingered only a minute after the federal officers left. "I'll keep you posted," he promised.

"Dennis, why don't you take the day off?" Nor suggested. "Pete can handle the bar."

"And lose all those holiday tips? I don't think so." Dennis yawned. "I better start setting up. We've got another holiday lunch group, Nor."

"I haven't forgotten. But they'll have to do without me. See you later."

When the door closed behind Dennis, Billy said, "Holiday tips? Forget it. He just wants to make sure that he's around if any trouble starts."

"I know. Are you going to try to get some sleep, Billy? Don't forget, we've got two more shows tonight."

"Right now I have to check my messages. I talked to a couple of the guys about getting together for lunch sometime this week."

Nor slipped her arm into her coat. "Hearing Hans Kramer's message was the reason we're in this mess. It would have been one thing if we could have stopped the fire, but now the prospect of being witnesses against those two scares me."

"Just remember they have no idea we overheard them." Billy pressed the playback button on the answering machine.

Sterling shook his head as he thought of Charlie Santoli. Maybe he won't mention that he saw Nor and Billy, he thought hopefully. But given the future events he already knew about, he was sure that wasn't the way things played out.

"You have two new messages," the electronic voice began.

The first was from a friend who was organizing a lunch for the next day. "You don't have to call back unless tomorrow doesn't work for you." The second was from the recording company executive who'd offered him the contract last night.

"Billy, this is short notice but Chip Holmes, one of our top guys, is coming into town unexpectedly. He would really like to meet with you today. He's staying at the St. Regis. Can you join us for a drink around 5:30? Let me know."

"Why do I think you can make it?" Nor asked when the message clicked off. "Chip Holmes. Billy, that's great. If Holmes likes you, the sky's the limit with that company. You won't just be another singer with potential. He'll put big money into building you up."

"Which is exactly what I need," Billy said, as he did a quick drumroll on the tabletop with his fingers. "I don't want to be a one-hit wonder. You know better than I do how many guys had a little success early on, and then ended up job hunting when they were thirty-five. Let's face it. In this business I'm already no kid."

"I know what you're talking about, but you're going to make it," Nor assured him. "Now I really will get out of here. Break a leg. I'll see you tonight."

At the door, she looked over her shoulder. "I always swear I won't give you advice, but I can't help myself. You'd better leave plenty of time to get into New York. The holiday traffic is still pretty heavy."

"I'll take the train," Billy said absently, as he picked up his guitar.

"That's smart."

When Nor left, Sterling settled back in the club chair, his legs stretched over the hassock. He listened as Billy began plucking at the strings and softly singing words he'd written on a crumpled sheet of paper.

He's trying out new lyrics, Sterling thought. Upbeat, but with a nice plaintive touch. Billy really is good. I always did have an ear for music, he recalled.

Forty-five minutes later, the phone rang. Billy picked it up, said, "Hello," listened, then said, nervously, "You're calling from Badgett Enterprises? What can I do for you?"

Sterling hoisted himself from the chair and in two quick strides was at Billy's side, his ear to the receiver.

At the other end of the line, Charlie Santoli stood in his office, hating himself more and more with every word he uttered. "I am a representative of the company. The reason I am calling is that, as you may know, the Badgett brothers are philanthropists who have a large scholarship program for children in the local area. They thoroughly enjoyed your performance last night, and they know you have a young daughter."

Sterling saw Billy's forehead tighten. "What has my daughter got to do with this?"

"Her future has a great deal to do with it. The Badgetts understand how uncertain your future as a performer may be. They would like to set up a trust fund to ensure that Marissa will be able to go to a fine college in another ten years."

"Why would they want to do that?" Billy asked, restrained anger in his voice.

"Because sometimes remarks made in jest are overheard and, if repeated, take on a life of their own. The Badgetts would be very upset if that happened."

"Are you threatening me?"

Of course I am, Charlie thought. It's my job. He cleared his throat. "What I am offering is to make your daughter one of the selected recipients of a one hundred thousand dollar trust fund. It would please Junior and Eddie Badgett very much if you'd accept. On the other hand, they would find it dismaying if you were to repeat lighthearted remarks that might be misconstrued."

Billy stood up. The receiver hit Sterling in the jaw, causing him to blink.

"Listen, you representative of Badgett Enterprises, whoever you are, you tell those two that my daughter doesn't need their trust fund. I'll take care of her education myself without any help from them . . . And as for their 'joking' or 'lighthearted' remarks, I don't have a clue what you're talking about."

He slammed down the phone, sank onto the couch, and clenched his hands into fists. "They know we heard them," he said aloud. "What are we going to do?"

The Heavenly Council was watching the developments on Earth with rapt attention. Charlie Santoli's phone call to Billy Campbell brought instant response.

"Charlie Santoli had better watch out," the monk said sternly.

"He'd better not come crying to us when his time is up." The shepherd's eyes flashed fire.

"It wasn't what the sisters taught him at St. Francis Xavier," the nun said sadly.

The queen's expression was grave. "He'd better wake up before it's too late."

"He wants to be good," the nurse volunteered.

"Well then, madam, for goodness sake, Charles Santoli must mend his ways and get on with it," the admiral thundered.

"I think Sterling will be looking to confer with us again," the Native American saint reflected. "He has great humility. He wants to do his job, and he's not afraid to ask for help."

"He was always capable of deep caring and love," the shepherd observed, his tone now mollified. "I was pleased by the expression in his eyes as he sat watching Marissa when she was sleeping."

Sterling caught up with Marissa just as she was putting her ice skates in her carrying case and rushing out to the car. When he had realized that Billy was going to catch a few hours' sleep, he had trotted over to Marissa's house to see how she was doing.

He arrived in time to join Roy as he drove Marissa to the rink, bringing the munchkins along for the ride. Squashed between the twins, Sterling ducked flailing arms that attacked him from both sides. His jaw was still a little sore from being bopped with the receiver when he'd been listening in on Santoli's conversation with Billy, and, at one year of age, Roy Junior had a mean right cross.

But they are cute babies, he conceded with only a shade of reluctance. It's kind of fascinating to see how they're taking in everything they see. My problem was that I didn't have any brothers or sisters. Maybe I wouldn't have been so anxious to stay away from kids all my life if I'd had some experience with them.

He remembered the time he was godfather at a christening and the baby had drooled all over his pin-striped suit. It was the first time I wore it, too.

In the front seat, Roy was saying to Marissa, "I understand Grandma is going to teach you how to make apple strudel today."

What a thrill, Sterling thought, and realized Marissa was having exactly the same reaction. However, she said politely, "I know. Grandma's so nice."

Roy smiled benignly. "I want to have at least *two* pieces."

"Okay, but don't forget I have to save a piece for Daddy and one for NorNor."

It's not easy to be a stepparent, Sterling thought sympathetically. Marissa always keeps him at arm's length. If I'd known Roy better before I met him next year, I wouldn't have been so quick to dismiss him as a bore.

But he does drive like a snail with a bad back. Sterling concurred totally with Marissa's impatient thought, "Step on it. Practice will be over before I get there."

She's Nor to a tee, Sterling decided.

When they arrived at the rink, Marissa thanked Roy for driving her, kissed him on the cheek, and waved to the twins before rushing out of the car.

Sterling climbed over Roy Junior's car seat and saw the surprised expression on the baby's face. He senses me, he thought. They both are beginning to sense me. Babies have so much awareness of the metaphysical. Too bad it gets lost along the way.

He caught up with Marissa and listened as she chatted animatedly with her friends at the side of the rink.

Miss Carr was the teacher he would see next year at the skating rink in Rockefeller Center. She blew a whistle and ten children, all the others a couple of years older than Marissa, skated onto the ice.

Some of the children were very good, but Marissa was simply outstanding. What a little trouper, Sterling thought as he watched her take a couple of hard spills. She just gets up, shakes herself off, and tries the spin or jump again.

Later, when the children had changed back into their shoes or boots, one of the girls came over to Marissa. "My sister got your dad's single for Christmas. She wondered if he would mind signing it for her."

Marissa's beaming with pride, Sterling thought as he watched and noted with amusement that she tried to sound oh-so-casual when she said, "Oh, sure. My dad likes to sign autographs for my friends."

"Is he writing a new song now?" the girl asked.

"He's always writing a new song."

"Tell him to write a song about us!"

"He's writing one about me first!" Marissa giggled.

Seven going on twenty-five, and bursting with love for her dad. Sterling sighed. And so near to being separated from him for a long time. Well, I've got to be off. He took one last look at Marissa's glowing smile, then left the rink.

Adjusting his homburg, he started walking back to Billy's apartment. He was planning to accompany him to his meeting, and was looking forward to being in Manhattan again.

But I'm really getting to know my way around Madison Village, he thought, as his feet crunched in the snow, making a sound only he could hear. I must say it's a very nice place to live.

"So howd'ya make out when you talked to Johnny one note?" Eddie asked. He was standing behind Junior, who, like a judge about to pass sentence, was sitting upright at his desk.

"Not very well." Charlie's hands were drenched in perspiration. He wanted to keep his voice calm but could not. "I spoke to Billy Campbell and offered him the scholarship for his daughter and explained that you would be dismayed if any remarks made in jest were misconstrued."

"All right, all right, we know what you were gonna say," Eddie said impatiently. "So what did he say?"

There was no staving off the answer. "He said for me to tell you that he'd pay for his daughter's education himself, and that he doesn't know what you mean by joking or lighthearted remarks. Then he slammed down the phone."

Charlie knew he could not soften Billy's reaction to the call, that if he tried, the brothers would see through him. The fact that Eddie was asking the questions was a frightening sign that now the next step would be taken. Coercion. And if that didn't work . . .

"Get out of here, Charlie," Junior ordered. "You sicken me. You let this happen." He looked up at his brother and nodded.

Charlie slunk out of the office. By tonight, Billy Campbell and Nor Kelly would have a warning that might frighten them into silence. Please let them take that warning seriously, he prayed, then shook his head in misery.

Once again he cursed the day fifteen years ago that the Badgett brothers had come to his one-man law office in Queens and asked him to represent them in their purchase of a dry-cleaning chain. I needed the business, so I didn't ask enough questions about them, he thought. Truthfully, I didn't want to know the answers. Well, I know them now.

When she reached home, Nor relaxed in the Jacuzzi, washed and blow-dried her hair, and, planning on a nap, dressed in lounging pajamas. Then Billy's phone call destroyed all thought of sleep.

Her throat closing, she listened as Billy related his conversation with "a representative of Badgett Enterprises."

"I called that FBI agent, Rich Meyers, and left a message for him. Then I called Sean, but he's out too. I waited to call you, Mom, because I hate to upset you, but you have to know what's going on."

"Of course I have to know about it. Billy, somehow those people found out that we were in that outer office. Maybe they have hidden cameras."

"Maybe. Or maybe someone spotted us coming out of there."

Nor realized she was trembling. "Do you know who it was on the phone?"

"He didn't give his name, but I think it might have been that guy who told us what to sing when we got there yesterday."

"I remember him. Kind of nervous and weasely-looking."

"That's the one. Look, I'd better get moving. I'm taking the three o'clock train into Manhattan."

"Billy, be careful."

"You're supposed to say, 'Break a leg.' "

"I already did."

"That's right, you did. See you later, Mom."

Mechanically, Nor replaced the receiver on the cradle. Break a leg. She had worked in a nightclub where the owner was behind in his payments to someone like the Badgetts. A broken leg had been his first warning to pay up.

And what didn't seem to have occurred to Billy yet was that the caller had talked about Marissa. Will the Badgetts try to get to Billy and me through Marissa? Nor agonized.

She dialed Sean O'Brien's number, hoping against hope that she'd reach him. He knew a lot about the Badgetts. Maybe he could tell her what they were likely to do next. We've already given statements, she thought. Even if we wanted to, how could we possibly take them back?

She knew the answer. It wasn't that they *couldn't* take them back. It was that they *wouldn't.*

I always used to dress in a suit when I had a business meeting, Sterling thought as he followed Billy onto the three o'clock train to Manhattan.

For his appointment with the recording company executives, Billy had chosen vintage jeans, a loose-fitting dark blue shirt, boots, and a leather jacket.

I'll never get used to these new styles. But then again, in the 1880s, when Mother was a young woman, she wore laced corsets, high-button shoes, bonnets, and floor-length dresses. Sterling sighed, suddenly nostalgic for the serenity of the afterlife, where concerns about clothing simply didn't exist.

He took the aisle seat next to Billy, who had found a vacant window seat. I always wanted the window seat too when I traveled by train, Sterling remembered. When Annie and I went to visit our friends in Westport, I always grabbed the window seat, and Annie never complained. I wonder if that's what the Heavenly Council meant when they called me "passive-aggressive"?

He could see how deeply worried Billy was just by looking at the troubled expression in his eyes and on his face. He was glad when Billy closed his eyes. Maybe he can relax a little, Sterling hoped. He's going to need to be "on" when he meets that guy Chip Holmes.

The train was a local and took forty-five minutes to get to Jamaica, in Queens. From there they took the subway to Fifty-ninth Street in Manhattan.

We're an hour early, Sterling noted as they climbed the steps to the street. Darkness was just setting in. The traffic was heavy, and there were Christmas decorations in all the windows. I hope Billy kills the time by taking a walk. I haven't been in this part of Manhattan in forty-six years.

It looks the same and yet different. Bloomingdale's will never change. But I don't see Alexander's. I loved living here, he remembered as he took it all in. There's no place like it in the world.

He trailed behind Billy to Park Avenue. The trees on the center island were glowing with white lights. The air was cold but clear. Sterling inhaled appreciatively even though it wasn't necessary for him to breathe. The hint of evergreen in the air made his mind drift back to other Christmases.

They started downtown and passed the building at 475 Park Avenue. My boss used to live there, Sterling recalled. He always invited Annie and me to his New Year's Day open-house party. Whatever happened to him? I never noticed him in the celestial waiting room and I never saw him whizzing by the celestial window.

Just then, a very old man, cane in hand, hobbled out of the building and spoke to the doorman. "My driver's late. Get me a cab, sonny."

Sterling gasped. It's him, my boss. Josh Gaspero. He must be a hundred years old! I'd love to be able to say hello, but from the looks of things, I suspect I'll be seeing him soon enough.

Billy was half a block ahead of him, and Sterling hurried to catch up, glancing over his shoulder several times as he watched his boss impatiently tapping his cane on the sidewalk. He hasn't changed, Sterling thought fondly.

The St. Regis was on Fifty-fifth Street, but Billy kept going south on Park Avenue. At Fiftieth Street he turned right and walked a few blocks west to Rockefeller Center.

Here I am again, Sterling thought. It's such a great place to be at Christmastime. I bet I know just where Billy's headed. Five minutes later they were in front of the magnificent evergreen with its thousands of colorful lights, looking down at the skating rink.

This is where it all started. Sterling smiled to himself. Started next year. Together they watched the skaters and listened to the music floating up from the rink. I'll bet Billy has skated here with Marissa. Sterling looked at the expression on Billy's face. I can tell she's in his thoughts right now.

Billy turned to leave. Sterling tailed him across Fifth Avenue and up the steps of St. Patrick's Cathedral. He's stopping to say a prayer, Sterling thought. The moment they walked through the door and experienced the majestic beauty of the cathedral, Sterling felt an intense sense of longing. His mind became filled with the image of the joy and peace he had seen on the faces of the people approaching the open gates of heaven. Head bowed, he knelt beside Billy, who had lit a candle at a side altar.

He's praying for his future on earth. I'm praying for mine in eternity. To be in heaven even for an hour on Christmas Day . . . Sterling felt tears in his eyes and whispered, "Please, help me complete my mission on earth so that I may begin to be worthy of You."

When they left St. Patrick's a few minutes later, Sterling was filled with both gratitude and regret. He knew that at last he was beginning to truly appreciate the gift of life and the gift of life everlasting.

At the St. Regis Hotel, Billy went into the King Cole bar, sat at a small table, and ordered a Perrier.

Oh, they've changed it here, Sterling thought as he looked around. But the Maxfield Parrish mural behind the bar is the same. I always loved it.

It was almost five o'clock. The bar was suddenly filling up. I remember meeting friends here for a glass of wine after work, Sterling mused. Just as people are doing now, getting together with friends, enjoying each other's company—that at least is timeless.

A couple of young women at a nearby table cast smiling glances at Billy, who was too absorbed in his own concerns to even notice them.

At five-twenty, Sterling could see that Billy was gearing up for the meeting. He straightened his shoulders, began sipping the Perrier, and kept his eye on the door. Ten minutes later, when the recording executive who had been at Nor's

Place appeared with a fast-moving, balding man in tow, Billy was the picture of easy charm.

They moved to a bigger table. But there's always room for one more, Sterling thought as he took the unoccupied seat and began to sort out his companions. It only took a moment to figure out that Chip Holmes was the top executive of the recording company, while Eli Green headed the New York office.

Holmes was a no-nonsense, say-it-and-be-finished-with-it type. "You're good, Billy, you're very good. You've got a special quality to your singing that makes me confident you'll catch on big time."

That's what I said, Sterling thought.

"You've got good looks, too, which is a rarity among the male performers in this business . . ."

Sterling silently applauded Billy's demeanor throughout the half-hour meeting. He looked and sounded confident, and, while appreciative, he did not grovel when Holmes offered a substantial contract and promised that he would have the kind of backup support he needed.

"We're teaming you with one of our top producers. He wants to get to work with you as soon as possible. By this time next year you could be a star, Billy."

The meeting ended with handshakes and a fervent expression of gratitude from Billy.

Good move, Sterling thought. During the discussion, you impressed him with your composure, but it was time to let him know how happy you are. I know his type. He loves having the role of kingmaker.

In the lobby, Billy consulted his train schedule and looked at his watch. Looking over his shoulder Sterling could see that he was going to try to make the 6:50 from Jamaica. A little tight, Sterling worried, but it's an express train, and the next one is a local.

They covered the seven blocks back to Fifty-ninth Street in half the time it had taken them to get to the hotel. Billy must be walking on air, Sterling thought. For the moment, at least. I'm sure that instead of thinking about the Badgetts, he's reveling in what the recording contract means to his future.

They hurried down the subway steps and onto the crowded platform. Consulting his watch again, Billy made his way to the edge and leaned forward, hoping to see a headlight emerging from the tunnel.

It happened in an instant. Sterling saw a burly man suddenly materialize, and with a slam of his shoulder send Billy teetering over the tracks. Anguished, Sterling tried to grab Billy, knowing that he could not regain his balance on his own, but his arms went right through Billy's body.

The train was rushing into the station. He's going to fall, Sterling thought helplessly. A woman screamed as the same burly man suddenly pulled Billy back to safety, then disappeared into the crowd, headed toward the exit.

The doors of the train opened. Numbly, Billy stepped aside as exiting passengers rushed past him.

"Are you all right?" someone asked him anxiously as he boarded the train.

"Yes, I'm all right." Billy grabbed the center pole near the door and held on tight.

An elderly woman admonished him. "Do you know how lucky you are? You should never stand that close to the edge of the platform."

"I know. It was stupid," Billy agreed, then turned away, struggling quietly to normalize his rapid breathing.

It wasn't stupid, Sterling wanted to shout, dismayed that he could not warn Billy. Billy doesn't realize he was pushed. The platform was so filled with people, he must think that the press of the crowd caused him to lose his balance, and that somebody grabbed him in time.

Sterling hung onto the center post with Billy as the subway bounced and swayed down the tracks. They arrived in Jamaica just in time to make the 6:50 to Syosset.

All the way home, chilling thoughts kept running through Sterling's mind: What happened on the subway platform was no accident, and what will the Badgett brothers do next?

Lee Kramer sat alone in the small hospital waiting room reserved for the families of people in intensive care. Except for the few minutes at a time that she had been able to stand at the foot of Hans's bed, this was where she had been since before dawn, when she had followed the ambulance to the hospital.

A massive heart attack. The words echoed dully in her mind. Hans, who in the twenty-two years of their marriage had hardly ever had a cold.

She tried to remind herself that the doctor had said that Hans was stabilizing. He said that Hans had been lucky. The fact that the fire department was at the scene and had the equipment to shock his heart and start it beating again had saved his life.

He's been under too much stress, Lee thought. The sight of the fire put him over the edge.

She glanced up when the door opened, then turned away. A number of her friends had stopped in and sat with her during the day, but she did not know this sober-faced, dark-haired man.

FBI agent Rich Meyers had come to the hospital hoping that he would be allowed to speak to Hans Kramer for a few minutes. That was out of the question, the nurse had told him firmly, but then added that Mrs. Kramer was in the waiting room.

"Mrs. Kramer?"

Lee whirled around. "Yes. Is anything . . . ? "

The strain on Lee Kramer's face was obvious. She looked as though she'd been punched in the stomach. Her short, ash-blond hair, blue eyes, and fresh complexion told Meyers that, like her husband, she was probably of Swiss extraction.

Rich introduced himself and handed her his card. A look of alarm came over her face. "FBI?" she asked.

"We're investigating the possibility that the fire at your husband's warehouse was deliberately set."

"Deliberately set? Who would do that?" Her eyes widened.

Meyers sat down in the vinyl chair opposite her. "Do you know anything about loans your husband may have taken out?"

Lee put her hand to her mouth, and the thoughts that had tormented her all day tumbled out. "When everything turned and the business started to go bad, we took a second mortgage on the house for every cent the bank would lend us. There's a mortgage on the warehouse, but only as much as we could borrow on it. I know it's underinsured. Hans was so sure that if he could tough it through a little longer, the business would take off. He really is brilliant. The software program he designed can't miss." Her voice faltered. "And now what does all that matter? If only he makes it . . ."

"Mrs. Kramer, in addition to the mortgages, were there any other loans your husband may have taken?"

"I didn't know about any, but this morning, after we got the call about the fire, he said something like, 'I borrowed a lot of money . . .' "

Meyers's face remained impassive. "Did he tell you who it was borrowed from?"

"No, that was all he said."

"Then you probably wouldn't have known if he made a phone call yesterday evening and left a message for someone about repaying a loan?"

"No, I don't know anything about that. But he was very agitated last night."

"Mrs. Kramer, does your husband have a cell phone?"

"Yes."

"We'd like to have your permission to check his cell phone account and home phone records to see if he made a call last night."

"Who would he have been calling?"

"People who don't give extensions on loans."

Her insides churning, Lee was afraid to ask the next question. "Is Hans in any trouble?"

"With the law? No. We just want to talk to him about that loan. The doctor will tell us when it's possible to see him."

"*If* it's possible," Lee whispered.

Charlie Santoli had left the Badgetts' office as quickly as possible after he'd been excoriated for not succeeding in his mission to buy Billy Campbell's silence, but at four o'clock Junior sent for him again.

He hastened down the corridor and around the corner to the executive suite shared by Junior and Eddie. Their long-time secretary was at her desk. Years ago, Charlie had decided that even as a baby, Lil must have had pugnacious features. Now that she had passed the fifty mark, they had settled into a permanent scowl. Still, he liked Lil, and she was probably the only person in the building who was not afraid of Junior.

She looked up, her eyes magnified by her oversized glasses, and jerked her thumb over her shoulder, always the sign to go right in. Then in a voice made hoarse by years of chain-smoking, she rasped, "The mood is slightly better." She paused. "Ask me if I care."

Charlie knew he didn't have to respond. He took a deep breath and pushed open the door.

Junior and Eddie were sitting on the zebra chairs, glasses

in their hands. Toward the end of the business day they often had a drink together before getting into their limo and heading home. If Charlie happened to be there, he was usually told to help himself from the bar.

Today was not one of those days. He was neither offered a drink, nor was he asked to sit down.

Junior looked over at him. "Just in case Campbell smartens up, we need to have this scholarship program on the level. Everyone knows we just gave big bucks to the old folks. Now we gotta take care of the little ones. You figure out the details. Find nine other outstanding kids from the area, all of 'em the age of Campbell's kid. We think it would be very nice of us to give them scholarships too."

They've got to be kidding, Charlie thought. Hesitantly, he suggested, "I think it would be wise if at least some of the children are older. How can you explain to the media that you want to give ten college scholarships to first-graders when there are high school boys and girls who need them now?"

"We don't wanna do that," Eddie barked. "We wanna build for the future. And if Campbell is smart enough to fall in line, we slide his kid's name in with the others."

"Marissa's marks are good and she's a nifty little ice-skater," Junior remarked offhandedly as he bit the end off a cigar. "Go find us other talented kiddies like her."

Charlie felt one more turn of the winch that twisted his digestive system. *Nifty little ice-skater.* How does Junior know so much about Marissa Campbell? he wondered bleakly.

"Of course, if you can't persuade Billy Campbell to retract anything he might have said about our little joke, there won't be any need for a fund," Junior said quietly. "Don't let us keep you, Charlie. I know how busy you are."

Back in his own office, Charlie tried to reassure himself that, bad as they were, people like Junior and Eddie never went after the children of their enemies.

But those two . . . He could not pursue the thought. Instead he found himself praying that Billy Campbell would wise up and accept the scholarship.

Shaking his head, he reached for a folder with the information about the car dealership the Badgetts wanted to buy. He had intended to spend his whole day on it, but had been too distracted to concentrate.

At 6:30 he closed the file and got up. He had his coat on and his briefcase in his hand when the phone rang. Reluctantly he picked it up.

A low, husky voice that he did not recognize said, "Charlie, the boss told me to pass the word that Billy Campbell almost took a dive in front of a subway train, but I managed to save him."

Before Charlie could answer, the connection was broken.

He replaced the receiver and stood at his desk for a long minute. In all the years he'd worked for the Badgetts, the worst he'd done was to speak to potential witnesses as he had spoken to Billy Campbell, and later arrange laundered payments to them. It had never gone beyond that. He could get the book thrown at him for tampering with witnesses, but this was different, and much more serious. They want me to be involved in whatever happens to Billy Campbell and Nor Kelly if I can't convince them to keep their mouths shut, he thought. I've never seen Junior and Eddie as foul tempered as they were today, and I know it's because they're worried.

He closed the door to his office and walked to the elevator. Even if Billy Campbell and Nor Kelly agreed to forget what they had overheard, would that be enough to ensure their safety?

Charlie doubted it.

Nor's Place was bustling when Billy and Sterling returned at eight o'clock. The dinner hour was in full swing and the bar was busy. Nor was talking to people at a table near the bar, but as though she had eyes in the back of her head, she turned around the instant Billy walked into the dining room. Her face brightened, and she hurried over to him.

"How did it go?"

Billy grinned. "Chip Holmes is crazy about the 'special quality to my singing.' "

He does a pretty good imitation of Chip Holmes, Sterling thought. He captures that nasal quality.

Nor threw her arms around him. "Oh, Billy, that's fantastic." She signaled to a nearby waiter. "Nick, we're celebrating. Bring us a bottle of Dom Perignon."

I wouldn't mind a glass of that, Sterling thought. As he took his usual seat at Nor's table, a host of memories rushed through his mind.

His mother and father opening a bottle of "Dom" on his twenty-first birthday . . .

Another "bit of the bubbly" shared with them when he passed the bar exam . . .

That wonderful crisp October day when he and Annie had driven with another couple to visit the Roosevelt home in Hyde Park. On the way back they stopped for a picnic lunch on the Palisades, and Annie had surprised everyone when she trotted out a chilled bottle of champagne and four glasses.

After I finished mine, I drank half of hers, he thought. Oh, Annie!

Sterling swallowed over a lump in his throat and realized he hadn't been paying attention to Billy and Nor. Obviously Billy had told her about the meeting, because she was saying, "Billy, that's wonderful! You're on your way."

None of them noticed that Sean O'Brien had come into the restaurant. They all looked up, surprised, when he joined them.

"Sorry I didn't get back to you earlier, Nor," he apologized. "Next time call me on my cell phone. Has anything else happened?"

"Tell Sean about the call from Badgett Enterprises, Billy," Nor said.

Sterling watched Sean O'Brien's expression darken as Billy related the scholarship offer.

When Billy shrugged his shoulders and said, "So that's it," Sean's first question was to ask if he had told the FBI about the call.

Billy nodded. "Rich Meyers wasn't in his office. I left a message."

"He called back here at about five o'clock," Nor said quietly. "My impression is that he thinks it was an iron fist in a velvet glove kind of warning."

O'Brien looked grim. "Listen, after being a detective for nearly thirty years, I know too much about these people. The iron fist will be front and center if you don't fall in line."

Billy, tell O'Brien about what happened in the subway, Sterling pleaded silently. You need protection.

"I guess we have no choice but to wait it out," Nor said. "Look, here's the champagne. On a happier note, we're drinking to Billy's future." She turned to him. "You'd better sip that fast. We have to go on pretty soon."

Billy got up. "I'll take it upstairs with me. I have to change, and I want to give Marissa a call. You know her. She wanted me to give her the scoop as soon as I got back."

I'll just wait here and keep Nor company, Sterling decided, when Dennis appeared from the bar.

"I wanted to congratulate Billy, but he's disappeared already."

"He went upstairs to change," Nor said.

Sterling listened as Nor happily filled the men in on Billy's meeting with the recording executives. Then she said, "The news about the contract is wonderful, but I can't tell you guys how tense I've been all day. Ever since Billy got that phone call, I've been so afraid of what the Badgetts might do next. . . . And right now I'd better get ready myself," Nor concluded. "We're on in fifteen minutes. Can you stay, Sean?"

"For a while. Kate's on duty tonight."

Dennis turned to Sean. "I've got to get back to work. Why don't you sit at the bar?"

As the group broke up, they all spotted Billy running down the stairs, a fire extinguisher under his arm.

"Mom, your car is on fire," he snapped. "I called 911."

Word of the fire spread through the dining room. Dennis grabbed a fire extinguisher from the bar. O'Brien and Sterling one step behind him, he raced outside to the blazing vehicle and, with Billy, tried to extinguish the flames.

Nor came out of the restaurant, surrounded by several diners whom she had been trying to calm.

Fire trucks came roaring into the parking lot, and immediately the firefighters ordered people to stand back.

It took only a few minutes for the fire to be extinguished. Nor's car had been in its usual spot near the kitchen entrance, well away from the general parking area.

Then Nor called, "Come on, everybody." She stood at the door, ushering people back into the restaurant.

When the hoses were turned off, the fire chief, Randy Coyne, accompanied by a Madison Village police officer, spoke to Nor, Billy, Sean, and Dennis privately in Nor's office.

"Nor, your car's a loss, but it could have been a lot worse. At least the fire didn't spread to any other vehicles, and I can tell you right now you're lucky it didn't spread to the restaurant."

"How did it start?" Nor asked quietly.

"We think it was doused with gasoline."

For a moment there was complete silence in the room, then Sean O'Brien said, "Randy, we have some idea of who's behind this, but it's a matter for the FBI. They're already investigating a telephoned threat Billy got this morning."

"Then call them immediately," the police officer said. "I'm going to make sure that we have a patrol car stationed here overnight."

"And one at Nor's house," Sean O'Brien said firmly.

"I'll be glad to know someone's keeping an eye out," Nor admitted.

Sean turned to Nor and Billy. "Nor, a piece of advice. The best thing you can do right now is for you and Billy to go out there and conduct business as usual."

"Wish I could stay for your show," the fire chief said with a half smile.

"I'll be outside until I can get someone posted here and at your home, Mrs. Kelly," the cop promised.

Billy waited until they were gone, then said slowly, "Something happened to me in the subway today. I really thought it was my own stupidity, but . . ."

Sterling watched the expressions on the faces of Nor, Dennis, and O'Brien become increasingly grave as Billy told them what had happened on the way home.

"The same guy who jostled you at the edge pulled you back," Sean said flatly. "That's an old trick with these people."

The phone rang. Billy answered it. He listened for an instant as the color drained from his face. Then, the receiver still in his hand, he said, "Someone just told me he's sorry he bumped into me on the platform, and maybe next time I should borrow my mother's car when I come in to New York."

An instant later in eternity, but one week later by the earthly calendar, Sterling requested and received a meeting with the Heavenly Council.

He sat in the chair facing them.

"You look as though you have the weight of the world on your shoulders, Sterling," the monk observed.

"I feel as though I do, sir," Sterling agreed. "As you know, the events of the past week moved rapidly after the car fire. The police and FBI convinced Nor and Billy that it was necessary to go into protective custody until the Badgett brothers' trial. The expectation was that the trial would take place in a relatively short time."

"We all know *that* won't happen," the shepherd said.

"Do you have a battle plan?" the admiral asked imperiously.

"I do, sir. I'd like to move through this earthly year quickly. I'm most anxious to get to the point where I meet Marissa and can start doing something to help her. My hands are tied until then. I'd just like to have glimpses along the way of what

I will need to know to assist me in safely reuniting Marissa with her father and grandmother."

"So you don't want to spend another full year on earth?" The queen sounded amused.

"No, I do not," Sterling told her, his voice solemn. "My earthly time is behind me. I'm impatient to help Marissa. She said good-bye to Nor and Billy only a few days ago, and already she's desolate."

"We're aware of that," the nurse said softly.

"Tell us your plan," the Native American saint suggested.

"Give me the freedom and the power to move through the year as quickly as I feel necessary, plus the ability to transfer myself from location to location by a simple request to you."

"Who are you planning to visit?" the matador asked.

"Mama Heddy-Anna, for one."

The Heavenly Council stared at him in shock.

"Better you than me," the monk muttered.

"Mama Heddy-Anna has put up with a lot," the nun said.

"I dread the day she shows up here," the admiral said. "I commanded ships in battle, but a woman like that, I must say, might just turn me into a coward."

They all laughed. The monk raised his hand, palm outward. "Go forward, Sterling. Do what needs to be done. You have our support."

"Thank you, sir." Sterling looked into the face of each of the eight saints and then he turned his head toward the window. The gates of heaven were so close he felt as though he could reach out and touch them.

"It's time to go, Sterling," the monk said, kindly. "Where do you want to be placed?"

"Wallonia."

"To each his own," the monk said and pushed the button.

A light snow was falling, the wind was cold, and the village of Kizkek looked as though it had been unchanged for a thousand years. It was in a little valley, nestled at the foot of snow-covered mountains that seemed to form a protective shield against the outside world.

Sterling found himself on a narrow street at the edge of the village. A wagon drawn by a donkey was approaching, and he stepped aside. Then he got a good look at the face of the driver. It was Mama Heddy-Anna herself, and she was hauling a load of logs!

He followed the wagon around the side of the house to the backyard. She stopped there, jumped down, tied the donkey to a post, and began to unload the logs, chucking them vigorously against the house.

When the wagon was empty, she unhitched the donkey and pushed it into a fenced-off section of the yard.

Stunned, Sterling followed Mama into the stone cottage. It appeared to be one fair-sized room built around a central fireplace. A large pot hanging over the fire was sending out the delicious smell of beef stew.

The kitchen area had a wooden table and benches. Mama's rocking chair was facing a television set, which stuck out like a sore thumb in its surroundings. A couple of other well-worn chairs, a hooked rug, and a scarred wooden cabinet completed the decor.

The walls were covered with photographs of Heddy-Anna's two offspring and her incarcerated husband. The mantel over the fireplace held framed pictures of several saints, obviously Mama's favorites.

While Mama pulled off her heavy parka and scarf, Sterling climbed the narrow staircase to the second floor. It contained two small bedrooms and a tiny bathroom. One room was clearly Mama's. The other had two side-by-side cots—obviously where Junior and Eddie laid their innocent heads during their formative years, Sterling decided. A far cry from the gaudy mansion on the north shore of Long Island they now inhabited.

The cots were piled with women's designer clothes, all with the tags still on. Clearly these were gifts from the missing sons, all items that their mother found absolutely useless.

Sterling could hear the faint sound of a phone ringing and hurried downstairs, immediately realizing that the Heavenly Council had given him a gift he hadn't thought to request. I never thought I'd see the day I could understand Wallonian, he reflected, as he heard Mama tell a friend to pick up some extra wine. Apparently there'd be ten of them for lunch and she didn't want to run short.

Oh good, Sterling thought. Company's coming. It's a great way to find out what Mama Heddy-Anna is all about. Then his eyes widened. She was speaking on a wall phone in the kitchen area. Next to the phone, where most people keep emergency numbers, there was a blackboard with a numbered list.

Probably a shopping list, he decided until he saw the words written in bold lettering across the top of the board:

ACHES AND PAINS

Sterling's eyes raced down the list:

1. Bad feet
2. Pains around heart
3. Gas
4. Dizzy spell
5. Threw up twice
6. Can't taste food no more
7. Need operation
8. Broken heart
9. Never close an eye
10. Bad back
11. Swollen gums

Now, I've seen it all, Sterling thought, as he noticed checks after each complaint, with dates of the brothers' phone calls from America. She's got this down to a science, he thought. She doesn't use the same complaint twice in a row.

Mama Heddy-Anna had hung up the phone and was standing next to him, examining the list with a satisfied smile.

Then, moving with the decisiveness of a drill sergeant, she began slinging dishes, glasses, and cutlery onto the table.

A few minutes later, her friends started to arrive. Wreathed in a smile, she greeted them with bear hugs.

She had said there would be ten of them. They're all very prompt, Sterling observed. The tenth guest was the one carrying the wine.

He guessed that they were all in their seventies and eighties and looked as if they had spent many years working outdoors. Their leathery complexions and callused hands were testimony to a lifetime of hard physical labor, but their ready laughter and joy in socializing was not different from that of the groups of friends Sterling had observed gathered at the King Cole bar in Manhattan, or at Nor's Place on Long Island.

Mama Heddy-Anna produced a steaming loaf of fresh-baked bread from the oven and dished out the stew. The wine glasses were filled, and everyone gathered at the table. Frequent bursts of laughter followed the exchanges of stories about their fellow villagers, or about outings they had enjoyed together. There had been a dance at the church hall the week before, and Heddy-Anna had done the Wallonian national folk dance on a tabletop.

"Now I want to dance on a tabletop at the monastery when they have their grand opening as a hotel on New Year's Day," Heddy-Anna announced.

"I skied over and took a look," the baby of the crowd, a sturdy seventy-year-old, said. "Can't believe how nice it is. It's been closed for twenty years, since the last monk left. It's nice to see it all fixed up."

"My boys used to ski over there all the time." Heddy-Anna helped herself to more beef stew. "Too bad the monastery is over the border. We could use the tourists' money here."

The peal of the telephone made them all giggle. Heddy-Anna wiped her mouth with her napkin, winked at her friends, put her finger to her lips, and waited for the fifth ring before answering feebly. "Ha . . . llllo."

She stood up to get a better look at the blackboard. "I can't hear. Talk louder. Wait, I gotta sit down. My foot's so bad today. It came out from under me. I laid on the floor all night. Finally managed to get up."

Her expression changed. "What'd'ye mean, 'Wrong number,' isn't this my Eddie?"

She slammed down the phone. "False alarm," she told her friends as she sat down and picked up her fork.

"It was good practice," the woman next to her said admiringly. "Heddy-Anna, believe me, you get better every time."

The phone rang again. This time Heddy-Anna made sure who she was talking to before she began to recite her list of complaints. She repeated almost verbatim the story she had told to the first caller. "And besides that . . ." she continued, tears in her voice.

The friend nearest the phone jumped up and pointed to item six on the list.

Heddy-Anna nodded. ". . . I can't taste a single bite of what I eat. The weight is dropping off me."

I guess I have the picture of what's going on in Wallonia,

Sterling thought wryly. Now I'd like to jump ahead to the next season and look in on Marissa.

He left the stone cottage, looked up at the mountains, then stared into the heavens.

May I please go back to Marissa's house? And let it be April, he requested, and then closed his eyes.

Spring comes first to the willows, Sterling thought as he looked at the slender and graceful clump of willow trees on the lawn outside Marissa's home in Madison Village. There was a pinkish haze about them, a promise of the blossoms that would soon be visible.

It was early evening, and dusk was just beginning to settle as the lingering rays of the sun disappeared. He went inside and found the family at the dinner table.

He took a chair in the dining room as far away as possible from Roy Junior and Robert, who were vigorously thumping their high chairs with spoons.

Marissa was sitting opposite them, silently picking at a small slice of chicken.

Denise and Roy were at the ends of the table, each one with the chair pushed close enough to the side so that they could easily feed a twin.

"How was school today?" Roy asked Marissa, as he managed to get a spoonful of mashed potatoes into Robert's mouth.

"It was okay, I guess," Marissa said listlessly.

"Marissa, you're just pushing the food around on your plate. You've simply got to eat something," Denise pleaded, then abruptly closed her lips after receiving a warning glance from Roy.

Marissa put down her fork. "I'm really not hungry. May I be excused?"

Denise hesitated, then nodded. "Daddy and NorNor should be phoning in an hour."

"I know."

"I'll call up to you, and you can go into our room and talk to them there."

Sterling was tempted to follow her but decided he wanted to hear what Denise would say to Billy when he called.

Denise waited until Marissa had disappeared up the stairs before speaking. "Roy, I couldn't bring myself to talk to her about the progress reports. She just can't seem to focus on her classes. The teacher said that she believes Marissa is blaming herself for Billy and Nor leaving, that Marissa thinks that somehow she did something wrong."

"A lot of kids feel like that when something happens to their parents, whether it's death, or divorce, or separation," Roy said. "We just have to be understanding."

Roy's a good soul, Sterling thought. He's trying very hard.

"Down, down, down." Roy Junior had had enough of sitting at the table.

"Down, down," Robert echoed, bouncing in his high chair.

Roy took a final bite of salad and got up. "Coffee later. I'll get these two upstairs and their baths started."

Denise began to clear the table. The phone rang a few minutes later. "Oh, Billy, you're early," she began. "No, of course, Marissa isn't out. If she knows you're going to call, she doesn't budge from the house for fear of missing you. Any new developments?"

She listened, then said, "Well, when you talk to her, tell her how proud you are that she's always been such a good student. We both know she'd do anything to please you. All right, I'll put her on. Give my best to Nor."

She laid the receiver on the table and walked to the staircase. "Marissa," she called.

Marissa was already at the head of the stairs. "Is that Daddy on the phone?"

"Yes."

Sterling hurried up the steps and followed Marissa's flying feet to the master bedroom. She closed the door tightly behind her.

For the next few minutes, Sterling listened as Marissa pleaded with Billy to come back. She promised she wouldn't *ever* pester to go to the movies, or try to make him stay on the phone and talk to her when she knew he was busy, or . . .

Sterling went over and bent down to listen to what Billy was saying. "Baby, don't even *think* like that! This has nothing to do with anything *you* did. I loved it when you phoned me . . ."

"Then why won't you tell me your phone number right now?" Marissa asked tearfully.

"Rissa, it's just that I can't. I have to borrow a phone when

I talk to you. NorNor and I want nothing more than to get home to you as soon as possible. Once I'm back, I'll make this all up to you, I promise . . ."

After she had finally said a tearful good-bye, Marissa went back to her room, sat at her desk, and turned on her CD player.

The sound of Billy's hit single filled the room. "I know what I want . . . I know what I need . . ."

Sterling watched as she put her head down on her arms and began to sob. I'm going to get you what you want and need, Marissa, Sterling vowed. And I'll do it if I have to move heaven and earth. No, with the *help* of heaven, he corrected himself.

He closed his eyes and addressed the Heavenly Council. Would you please deliver me to wherever the Badgett brothers are at the moment?

When Sterling opened his eyes, he found himself inside a large, bustling, noisy restaurant on the water.

Unless the brothers are traveling, I guess that's Long Island Sound, he thought. He looked over at a woman studying the menu. The cover read SAL'S ON THE SOUND.

It was a steak-and-seafood place. People with bibs were happily breaking lobster claws; sirloin steak on sizzling platters was obviously popular. And, he noticed, many diners had chosen his favorite appetizer, crabmeat cocktail.

But where were Junior and Eddie? He was on his second tour of the tables when he noticed a secluded semicircular corner booth with a prime water view. Upon closer inspection he saw the three occupants were none other than Junior, Eddie, and a scantily clad Jewel.

Junior and Eddie had just had one of their telephone visits with Mama Heddy-Anna, and as usual both of them were in a tailspin worrying about her. Jewel had suggested they'd all feel much, much better if they went out for a nice, relaxing dinner.

They were already sipping cocktails, and the waiter was in the process of collecting the menus.

Sterling took a seat on the windowsill at a right angle to them. I wonder what they ordered? he thought.

"I don't think I can eat a bite," Eddie lamented. "When I think of how sick Mama is, I'm crying inside."

"You've been crying outside too, Eddie," Jewel said. "Your nose is all red." She patted Junior's hand. "Yours is red too, lambie."

Junior pushed her hand away. "I have a cold."

Jewel realized her mistake. "And your allergies, honey. The allergy season is terrible right now. This is the worst it's been in years."

"Yeah, yeah." Junior picked up his glass.

"She fell again," Eddie mourned. "Our poor mama's foot gave way again, and on top of that, her gums are swollen. She can hardly chew."

I guess she didn't use that one last time, Sterling thought.

"And her friends keep begging her to eat. Nothing tastes good to her anymore."

"She's been saying that ever since I met you guys three years ago," Jewel said earnestly. "She must be eating *something.*"

Beef stew, Sterling thought. Lots of beef stew.

"She hasn't fallen since January," Eddie continued. "I was hoping her legs were getting better." He turned to Junior. "We gotta go see our mama. I'm telling you we gotta go see her."

"We can't and you know it," Junior snapped. "We sent her some nice new clothes to cheer her up."

"She's gonna love them," Jewel enthused. "I picked them out special. Two pairs of satin lounging pajamas, a cocktail dress, and a hat with lots of flowers to wear to church on Easter Sunday."

Eddie's expression soured. "Mama says the clothes we send her stink."

"That hurts my feelings," Jewel said, pouting. "If I met her, I'd be able to shop for her better. Every woman has figure problems. I mean it could be her hips, it could be her waist, her behind might have a funny shape—"

"Shut up, Jewel," Junior thundered. "I don't want no more anatomy lessons."

I was enjoying it, Sterling thought.

Obviously offended, Jewel got up. "Please, excuse me," she said with exaggerated emphasis.

"Where yuh goin'?" Eddie asked.

"To the lala." She flounced away.

"Is she mad because I said Mama don't like the clothes she picked out?"

"Forget the clothes," Junior barked. "Listen, I got a call when *you* were in the lala."

"When was I in the lala?"

"You're always in the lala."

"No, I'm not."

"Yes, you are. Every time I go look for you, you're in the lala. Now listen to me. Our guys can't track down Nor Kelly and Billy Campbell."

"They're a bunch of dopes," Eddie said.

"It takes one to know one. Keep your mouth shut and listen to me. The whole case against us falls apart if Kelly and Campbell don't take the stand. We gotta get rid of them."

"It's a big country. How do we get rid of them when we can't find them?"

"We gotta find them. I took the next step. I called a certain hit man."

Eddie looked at Junior. "Not Igor?"

"Yes, Igor," Junior said. "He's very good at what he does. I told him the only lead we have so far is that they're somewhere out West."

"Here I am," Jewel chirped as she slid into the banquette and kissed Junior's cheek. "I've forgiven you both for not appreciating all I do to make Mama Heddy-Anna happy and comfortable, and I have to tell you something. I think you should figure out a way to go visit your mama in person, and you should do it before it's too late."

Junior glared at her. "Drop it."

The waiter appeared with a tray of appetizers.

I've learned what I needed to know, Sterling thought. The Badgett brothers are determined to track down Nor and Billy and make sure they don't live to testify against them.

Sterling decided to take a long walk before he made a request to be transported somewhere else. An hour later, he had made his decision. He closed his eyes and whispered, I'd like it to be midsummer, and may I please get together with Nor and Billy?

Surely they're not staying *here,* Sterling thought, dismayed. He was standing on the second-floor balcony of a rundown motel directly off a busy highway. Although it was blazing hot, the area was beautiful. Like Mama Heddy-Anna's village, the landscape boasted magnificent mountain views.

Of the six vehicles parked outside the motel, four had Colorado plates.

He noticed a heavyset man with dark glasses sitting in an SUV. It seemed to Sterling that the man was staring at his rearview mirror, watching the door directly behind him.

Sterling turned and peeked in the window. Billy was standing inside the shabby room, hands in pockets. He was looking at Nor, who was sitting on the edge of the bed, a phone in her hand.

They looked different. Nor's blond hair was medium brown, and she wore it in a prim knot at the nape of her neck. Billy had a beard, and his dark hair was cut much shorter.

Maybe this is where they make their calls home, Sterling thought. If they're in the Witness Protection Program, they can only phone from secured lines. They both look worried sick.

He went inside, and taking off his homburg, put his ear to the receiver. I'm getting good at eavesdropping, he thought. He heard a familiar voice at the other end of the line and realized that Nor was talking to Dennis.

"Nor, I don't have to tell you that this place is all about you," Dennis was saying. "Sure, I can do drinks, and the guys are good waiters, and Al is the best chef we've ever had, but that's not good enough. When the customers come in, they want to see you at your table."

"I know. How big a loss this month?"

"Very big. We're not a quarter full for dinners, even on Saturdays."

"Which means, of course, that the waiters' tips are way down," Nor said, "Look, Dennis, this can't last much longer. The minute the trial is over and the Badgetts are in prison, we'll be able to come home. Figure out how much in tips the guys are losing, and let's make up half of it to them in their paychecks."

"Nor, maybe you didn't hear me. You're losing money hand over fist as it is."

"And maybe you didn't hear me," Nor flared. "I know the restaurant needs me to be there. But you and Al and the waiters and the kitchen help and the cleanup crew are all part of what make it work. It took me years to put together such a good team, and I'm not going to lose it now."

"Take it easy, Nor, I'm just trying to help you keep your head above water with this place."

"I'm sorry, Dennis," Nor said contritely. "This whole business is grinding me down."

"How's Billy?"

"How do you think? He just called Marissa and the recording company. Marissa absolutely refuses to talk to him—or to me either for that matter—and the recording company told him that unless this is over soon, they'll have to cancel his contract."

There was silence, then Nor said, "Dennis, you know that impressionist painting near the fireplace in my living room?"

"The pain-by-numbers one?"

It was an old joke between them.

"Yes. You have power of attorney. Go to my safe-deposit box and get the papers on it. Take everything to the Reuben Gallery. I know they'll make an offer on it. It should be worth at least sixty thousand dollars. That will help."

"You love that painting, Nor."

"Not as much as I love my restaurant. Okay, Dennis, I guess that's all the good news I can handle at one time. I'll talk to you in about two weeks."

"Sure, Nor. Hang in there."

Her next call was to Sean O'Brien to see if there was any word about the trial date. There wasn't.

They left the motel room in silence, went down the steps to the parking area, and got into the SUV in which the man in dark glasses was sitting. He's got to be the federal marshal who looks out for them, Sterling decided.

He rode in the backseat with Nor. Not a word was exchanged on the twenty-minute drive. He spotted a road sign that indicated Denver was thirty miles away. I know exactly where we are, he thought. The Air Force Academy is near here.

Billy and Nor were living in a run-of-the-mill bi-level house, the sole virtue of which, at least as far as Sterling could tell, was its location. It was set on a large piece of property, shaded by tall trees that afforded privacy.

When the car stopped, Billy turned to the marshal. "Frank, come inside please. I've got to talk to you."

"Sure."

The living room furniture looked as if it had been purchased at the auction of a bankrupt motel: Naugahyde sofa and chairs, mismatched Formica coffee and end tables, burnt-orange wall-to-wall carpeting. A groaning air conditioner labored to pump in cool air.

Sterling could pick out Nor's attempts to make the room livable. Tasteful framed prints drew the eye away from the hideous furnishings. A vase of black-eyed susans and several large green plants helped alleviate the depressing atmosphere.

The living room opened into what was meant to be a dining area. Billy had turned it into a music room, furnishing it with a scarred upright piano piled with sheet music, a CD player, and shelves of CDs. His guitar rested on a club chair near the piano.

"What can I do for you, Billy?" the marshal asked.

"You can help us pack. I'm not staying here another night. I've had it."

"Billy, this is not Frank's fault," Nor said, hoping to placate him.

"For all we know, this trial will never happen. Am I supposed to spend the rest of my life rotting in this house? Frank, let me explain something to you. I turned thirty years old last week. In the music business that's old, you understand? It's *old.* The ones who make it these days, start at seventeen, even younger."

"Billy, calm down," Nor begged.

"I can't calm down, Mom. Marissa is growing up without us. She's growing up *hating* me. Every time I talk to Denise she tells me how worried she is about Rissa, and she's right. I'm taking my chances. If anything happens to me, at least it will happen while I'm living my own life."

"Listen, Billy," the marshal interrupted. "I know how frustrating this is for you and for your mother. You're not the first one in this program who's gone crazy. But you *are* in real danger. We have ways of finding out things. There was no reason to tell you this before, but there's been a contract on you and your mother since January. And when the Badgetts' personal goons couldn't find you, they hired a hitman."

Nor paled. "When did they hire him?"

"Three months ago. We know who he is and our men are looking for him. Now, do you still want me to help you pack?"

The fire went out of Billy. "I guess not." He walked over and sat at the piano. "I guess I'll just keep writing music that somebody else will have the chance to sing."

The marshal nodded to Nor and left. After a few moments,

Nor went over to Billy and put her hands on his shoulders. "This really won't last forever, you know."

"It's hell on earth."

"I agree."

I do too, Sterling thought. But what do I do about it? The more he learned about the problem, the less he felt able to solve it.

With a sympathetic glance at Nor and Billy, he went outside. I'm used to the altitude in the heavens, but not in Colorado, he thought, feeling a little light-headed.

It's hard to believe that Nor and Billy will still be here in December. I can only imagine the emotional state they'll be in by then. Where else can I go? What can I do? Everything hinges on the trial. Maybe I should drop in on the Badgetts' legal counselor. After all, he was the one who saw Billy and Nor coming out of Junior's office.

I'll be glad to get out of this heat, Sterling decided as he closed his eyes. Summer was always my least favorite season.

Once more he addressed the Heavenly Council. May I please be transported into the presence of Charlie Santoli, and may it please be in early December? Amen, he added.

"We should have put the lights up at least a week ago," Marge commented as she unrolled another string of bulbs and handed them to Charlie, who was standing on a ladder outside their living room window.

"I've been too busy, Marge. I just couldn't get to it." Charlie managed to loop the string over the top of the evergreen, which had grown considerably taller since last year. "You know, there are people we can pay to do this. They have higher ladders, they're younger, they're stronger, and they could do a better job."

"Oh, but then we'd miss out on all the fun, Charlie. We've been doing this together for forty years. The time will come when you really can't do it, and then you'll wish you could. Admit it. You love this ritual."

Charlie smiled reluctantly. "If you say so."

Sterling sat on the steps observing the couple. He really is enjoying himself. He's a family man, he thought.

An hour later, chilled but pleased with themselves, Marge and Charlie went into the house, shed their coats and gloves, and gravitated to the kitchen for a cup of tea. When the teapot and freshly baked Christmas cookies were in front of them, Marge dropped her bombshell.

"I want you to quit that job with the Badgett brothers, Charlie, and I want you to quit it tomorrow morning."

"Marge, are you out of your mind? I can't do that."

"Yes, you can. We're not rich, God knows, but we've got enough to live on. If you want to keep working, put out your shingle again and do house closings and wills. But I'm not putting up with watching you build to a heart attack working for the Badgetts for another day."

"Marge, you don't understand—I can't quit," Charlie said desperately.

"Why not? If you drop dead, they'll get a new lawyer, won't they?"

"Marge, it's not that. It's . . . please, let's just forget it."

Marge stood up and placed both hands firmly on the table. "Then what is it?" she asked, her voice rising with every word. "Charlie, I want the truth. What's going on?"

Sterling listened as Charlie, at first hesitantly, then in a rush of words, confessed to his wife that over the years he had been sucked into making threats to people who stood in the way of the Badgetts. He watched Marge's reaction change from horrified shock to deep concern as she came to realize how emotionally tortured her husband had been for years.

"The trial I've been getting postponed has to do with the warehouse fire near Syosset last year. The singers hired for that Mama Heddy-Anna birthday party overheard Junior giving the order to have it torched. The word on the street is that the entertainers are working in Europe, but the truth is they're in protective custody."

So that's the story that's been circulated about Nor and Billy, Sterling thought.

"Why do you want the trial postponed?"

"We bribed experts who will swear the fire was caused by exposed wires. Hans Kramer, the guy who owned the warehouse, disappeared, but the brothers found out last month that he and his wife are living in Switzerland. They've got family there, and after what happened, Kramer doesn't want to tangle with the Badgetts."

"You haven't answered my question, Charlie."

"Marge, I'm not the one who wants the postponements. The Badgetts want them."

"Why?" She looked straight into his eyes.

"Because they don't want the trial to start until Nor Kelly and Billy Campbell are silenced for good."

"And you're going along with that?" she asked incredulously.

"They may not find them."

"And they *may* find them. Charlie, you can't let that happen!"

"I know I can't," he burst out. "But I don't know what to do. You must realize that the minute I go to the feds, the Badgetts will know it. They have a way of finding out those things."

Marge began to cry. "How did this happen? Charlie, no matter what the consequences for us, you have to do the right thing. Just wait a few more days until Christmas is over. Let's have one more Christmas when we know we'll all be together." She wiped her eyes with the back of her hand. "I'll pray for a miracle."

Charlie stood up and wrapped his wife in his arms. "Well, when you say your prayers, be more specific," he said with a tired smile. "Pray for a way to make Junior and Eddie visit Mama Heddy-Anna in the old country. I can have the cops ready to nab them the minute they set foot on Wallonian soil. Then we'd all be in the clear."

Marge looked at him. "What are you talking about?"

"They've been tried in absentia for the crimes they committed over there and both got life sentences. That's why they can never go back."

Life sentences! Sterling thought. At last he understood what he had to get done. The only question was how to do it.

Sterling went outside. Marge had turned on the Christmas lights as soon as Charlie finished hanging them. The weather was changing, and the late afternoon sun had disappeared behind heavy clouds. The multicolored bulbs on the evergreen twinkled cheerily, helping to dispel the growing gloom of the winter day.

Suddenly, like a gift, Sterling remembered something he had overheard at Mama Heddy-Anna's lunch table. It's possible, he thought, it's possible. A plan to get the brothers back to the old country began forming in his mind.

It was a long shot, but it just might work!

"Sterling, it looks as if you've been doing your homework," the nun said approvingly.

"You're quite the world traveler," the admiral boomed.

"We were surprised that you went back to Wallonia," the monk told him, "but then we got an inkling of what you were up to. That was my old monastery, you know. I lived there fourteen hundred years ago. Hard to believe it's being turned into a hotel. I can't imagine that place having room service."

"I can understand that, sir," Sterling agreed, "but for our purposes it may be most fortuitous. I think I have at last found a way to help Marissa and Nor and Billy, and maybe even Charlie. He needs my help as much as Marissa does, but in a different way."

He squared his shoulders and looked into one face after the other. "I request permission to appear to Charlie so that he can work with me on solving the problems."

"Do you mean to appear as you did to Marissa, who understood you were not of her world?" the shepherd inquired.

"Yes. I think that's necessary."

"Perhaps you'd better plan to become visible to Marge as

well," the queen suggested. "Something tells me she rules the roost in that family."

"I was afraid to push the envelope and ask to meet her," Sterling admitted with a smile. "It would be wonderful if I could communicate with both of them."

"Push the envelope?" The matador's eyebrows raised. "That expression wasn't in vogue when you were alive."

"I know. But I heard it somewhere. Maybe in Nor's restaurant. I kind of like it." He stood up. "According to the earthly calendar, tomorrow will be the day when I first met Marissa. I've come full circle."

"Don't forget, it was also the day you first appeared before us," the Native American saint teased.

"That, I assure you, I'll never forget."

"Go forward with our blessing," the monk told him. "But remember—Christmas Day, which you hope to celebrate in heaven, is drawing very near."

Marissa opened the door of her room and was delighted to see Sterling sitting in the big chair by the desk. "I thought you were going away and would come back to say good night," she said.

"I did go away," he explained. "I took a look at the whole last year of your life when you were down at dinner and understand now why Daddy and NorNor had to leave."

"But I've only been downstairs for an hour!"

"Time is different for me," Sterling said.

"I kept thinking about you. I ate fast, then got stuck listening to Roy tell his boring story about Christmas when he was a little boy and was one of the shepherds in the school play. I got away as fast as I could. I'm so glad you're here."

"Well, I learned a lot while you were at dinner. I'm going to have to leave now because I'm going to be very busy trying to get your daddy and NorNor back for your birthday."

"That's Christmas Eve," she reminded him quickly. "I'll be eight years old."

"Yes, I know."

"That's only four days from now."

Sterling saw skepticism mixed with hope in Marissa's eyes. "You can help me," he told her.

"How?"

"Say a few prayers."

"I will. I promise."

"And be nice to Roy."

"It isn't easy." Her whole personna changed, and her voice deepened. " 'I remember the time when . . . blah, blah, blah.' "

"Marissa," Sterling cautioned, with a twinkle in his eye.

"I knowwwwww . . ." she said. "Roy's all right, I suppose."

Sterling stood, relishing the momentary lightheartedness he saw in Marissa's eyes. It was an instant reminder of the first time he had seen her with Billy and Nor. I cannot fail her, he thought. It was both a prayer and a vow.

"It's time for me to go now, Marissa."

"Christmas Eve—you promised!" she said.

Charlie and Marge always piled the presents under the tree a few days before Christmas. Their three children all lived nearby on Long Island, a blessing for which Marge gave daily thanks.

"How many people's kids are scattered to the ends of the earth?" she would ask rhetorically from under the dryer. "We're so lucky."

Their six grandchildren were a source of joy, from the seventeen-year-old about to start college to the six-year-old in the first grade. "All good kids. Not a lemon in the lot," Marge often boasted.

But tonight, after she and Charlie had arranged the gifts, they did not feel their usual sense of satisfaction and anticipation. Dread of the inevitable outcome of Charlie going to the FBI had settled over them, and at 8:30 they were sitting quietly side by side in the living room, Charlie aimlessly flipping the channels on the television.

Marge stared at the Christmas tree, a sight that usually brought her great comfort and joy. Tonight it didn't have that effect on her. Not even the homemade ornaments her grandchildren had made over the years could bring a smile to her face.

Then, as she watched, one of the ornaments slid to the carpet, the paper-mâché angel with one wing shorter than the other, and wearing a hat instead of a halo. She got up to retrieve the angel, but before she could reach it, the ornament started to glow.

Her eyes widened. Her jaw dropped. For once, not a word came from her lips. In ten seconds the angel had been transformed into a pleasant-faced man, neatly dressed in a dark blue chesterfield coat and wearing a homburg, which he promptly removed.

"AAAAAAAAAHHHHHHHHHH," Marge screamed.

Charlie had started to doze on the couch. He jumped up, saw Sterling, and cried, "Junior sent you, I know he did."

"Jesus, Mary, and Joseph," Marge cried prayerfully. "The Badgetts didn't send him, Charlie. He's a ghost."

"Please don't be alarmed. I'm here to help solve your problems with the Badgetts," Sterling said calmly. "Do sit down."

They looked at each other and then obeyed. Marge blessed herself.

Sterling smiled. For a moment he said nothing, wanting them to get used to him and lose any lingering fear that he might do them harm.

"Mind if I sit down?" he asked.

Marge's eyes were still like saucers. "Please do, and help yourself to the Christmas cookies," she said, pointing to the dish on the coffee table.

"No, thank you." He smiled. "I don't eat anymore."

"I wish I had that problem," Charlie said, staring at Sterling, the remote control still in his hand.

"Turn off the TV, Charlie," Marge ordered.

Click. Sterling was amused, remembering the queen's remark that in this house, Marge ruled the roost. He could see them both begin to relax. They understand that I'm not here to harm them, he thought. It's time to explain myself to them.

"You know Nor Kelly and Billy Campbell, Charlie," he began. "And you know they are in the Witness Protection Program."

Charlie nodded.

"I was sent here to help Billy's little girl, Marissa, who longs to be with her father and grandmother. In order to accomplish that, it is necessary to remove the threat that hovers over them."

"Junior and Eddie," Charlie said flatly.

"Those two!" Marge said contemptuously.

"As I began investigating the best way to ensure Nor and Billy's safety, I realized that you are in grave danger from the Badgetts as well."

Marge reached for Charlie's hand.

"Understanding all the circumstances, I have come to the conclusion that the best and most effective way to solve the problem is to get the Badgetts to go back to Wallonia, where they will be incarcerated for the remainder of their lives."

"And I hope they throw away the key," Marge pronounced. "Those two are bad, bad, bad."

Ever the lawyer, Charlie said, "I assure you, there is no way that those two will ever willingly set a foot on Wallonian soil."

"Even for Mama Heddy-Anna?" Sterling asked.

"They've been crying in their beer for nearly fifteen years about not seeing her, but they still haven't paid her a visit," Charlie said.

"I have a plan that just might take them back to their mother's side," Sterling explained.

Their expressions suddenly hopeful, Charlie and Marge listened raptly.

The next morning, FBI agent Rich Meyers, accompanied by his top assistant, agent Hank Schell, arrived at the home of Charlie and Marge Santoli. Dressed as repairmen, they carried in tool kits that held recording equipment.

They sat at the kitchen table with the Santolis while Schell set up and tested the microphone.

When Charlie had phoned Meyers the previous night, Meyers warned him that he might want to have legal counsel before going on the record with potentially self-incriminating disclosures.

Charlie had dismissed the suggestion. I've got something far better than a lawyer, he thought. I've got Sterling in my corner.

"Ready, Mr. Santoli?" Meyers asked.

"Yes, I am. For the record, my name is Charles Santoli . . ."

For the next hour, Charlie described his connection with the Badgetts, starting with their legitimate enterprises, then detailing his growing knowledge of their criminal activities. He concluded by saying that in his opinion the government would never be able to convict Junior and Eddie Badgett of arson in the Kramer warehouse fire, and that Nor Kelly and Billy Campbell would always be in grave danger, whether or not they were in protective custody.

Meyers listened impassively.

Charlie took a deep breath. "With what I'm going to suggest to you, you may decide I need medication, not legal help, but at least hear me out."

Sterling made a face at Charlie and winked.

With a slight smile, Charlie calmly laid out the plan Sterling had outlined to him the night before. Every once in a while he glanced over at Sterling for approval and was rewarded with an encouraging nod.

Meyers' first reaction—"You want to do *what*?"—gradually changed to a grudging "It's not impossible," to an eventual "We've spent thousands of hours trying to get these guys and haven't been able to make anything stick. But if they're in prison for good, in Wallonia, their whole rotten operation will fall apart."

"That's my point," Charlie said eagerly. "It may take years to get a conviction here, and even in prison, they'd still be dangerous. But put them in prison halfway around the world, and those dopey goons of theirs would just disappear."

When the recorder was turned off, the two agents stood up, and Meyers said, "Obviously I've got to talk to the big guys at the office about this. I'll get back to you in a couple of hours."

"I'll be here," Charlie said. "My office is closed through Christmas."

When Meyers and Schell left, Marge commented, "Waiting is always the hardest part, isn't it?"

Sterling thought of his forty-six years in the celestial waiting room. "I absolutely agree," he said. "Hopefully the waiting will be over very soon for all of us."

At one o'clock, Rich Meyers phoned back. "It's a go. If you can do your part, we'll take care of the rest."

"The stores are always so busy at Christmastime," Jewel sighed as the limo pulled through the gates of the Badgett estate at three o'clock. "But doesn't it get you into the spirit, going to the mall and seeing everybody rushing around, doing their last-minute shopping?"

"It gets on my nerves," Junior said sourly. "I don't know how you talked me into going."

"Me too," Eddie echoed. "I'm not the type to eat lunch in the food court. That place was so noisy, I couldn't hear myself think."

"You never think anyway," Junior muttered.

"Very funny," Eddie growled. "Everybody says I take after you."

"But we got some good stuff," Jewel said brightly. "Those ski sweaters I treated you to look so nice. The trouble is we never go away, and there's not much skiing on Long Island." She shrugged her shoulders. "Oh, well. What're you gonna do?"

Inside the house, Jewel went straight to the salon to plug in the Christmas tree. "I can't say I'm crazy about all these purple lights," she murmured as she squatted, cord in hand, fishing for the outlet.

Junior was at the window. "You invite one of your ditzy friends over here, Jewel? There's a car down at the gate."

"My friends aren't ditzy, and no, they're all out shopping."

The intercom rang. Eddie went to the security panel on the wall and pushed the button. "Who is it?"

"It's Charlie, and I have my wife with me. Mind if we come up for a few minutes?"

Eddie rolled his eyes. "Sure, I guess it's okay."

"What the heck is Charlie bringing Marge over here for?" Junior asked irritably.

"It's the holidays," Jewel reminded them. "People drop in and visit each other. No big deal. Just nice and friendly. And caring."

"The holidays stink," Eddie said. "They make me feel bad."

"That's a very natural reaction," Jewel told him earnestly. "I was just reading an article written by a very smart psychologist. According to him, people get depressed because—"

"Because people like you drive them crazy," Eddie interrupted.

"Watch it, Eddie. Jewel is only trying to cheer us up."

"Oh, lambie pie, you're so right. That's all I want to do."

Eddie went to the door to admit the Santolis.

As the handle turned, Sterling whispered, "Don't be nervous, Marge."

Eddie's lame greeting, "Hi yah, come on in," made both Santolis know exactly how welcome they really were.

Marge braced herself and followed Eddie into the salon, trailed by Charlie and the ever-present Sterling.

"Welcome," Jewel trilled. "Happy holidays. What a nice surprise. We were thrilled to see your car drive in."

Oh my God, look at that tree, Marge thought. The few times she'd been in this house around Christmas, the trees had been reasonably traditional. Not this year.

She was holding a tin of cookies and handed it to Jewel. "I make these for all my friends every Christmas," she said.

"A sign of love," Jewel cooed.

"Sit down for a minute," Junior said. "We were on our way out."

"Sit, sit, sit," Jewel encouraged.

"We won't stay," Charlie promised as he and Marge sat together on a couch. "It's just that Marge had a dream last night that was so powerful, she felt she had to alert you."

"Alert us about what?" Junior asked, his tone measured.

"I had the most disturbing dream last night—about your mother," Marge began.

"MAMA!" Eddie bellowed. "Did something happen to her?"

Marge shook her head. "No, but does she suffer from dizzy spells?"

"Yeah," Junior's eyes bored into Marge's face.

"Pains around the heart?"

"Yeah."

"Gas?"

"Yeah."

"She can't taste her food?"

"Yeah."

"Never closes an eye?"

"Yeah."

"Throws up occasionally?"

"Yeah."

"Swollen gums?"

"I can't take it no more," Eddie shouted, his face crumbling into tears. "I gotta call her."

He ran to the phone.

Mama Heddy-Anna's annual Christmas party was in full swing. The wine and grappa were flowing. Everybody had brought a favorite dish, and the table was groaning with food. An old phonograph was scratching out Christmas carols, and a sing-along was in full swing.

When the phone rang, the person nearest to the phonograph yanked the needle from the record and screamed, "Pipe down, everybody!"

A few additions to Mama's list of ailments had been added by a couple of the partygoers, and someone obligingly pointed them out, as after waiting for the fifth ring, Mama Heddy-Anna picked up the phone.

"Ha . . . Ha . . . lllo."

"Mama, how are you? Someone had a dream you weren't feeling so good . . ."

"They dreamed right." Heddy-Anna winked at her friends

and motioned for her eyeglasses as she squinted at the new writing on the board.

"Mama, talk louder, I can't hear you. You sound so sick . . ."

Heddy-Anna read from the blackboard. "I think this is my last Christmas." She sighed, then improvised: "Did the person with the dream warn you that I'm a dying woman?"

"Mama, don't say that. It's not true. Grandmama lived to be one hundred and three, remember."

"She was a strong woman . . . not like me."

Junior picked up the extension. "Mama, is something worse?"

"I threw up this morning . . . because my gums are so swollen . . . dizzy, you should know how dizzy I am . . . can't see straight . . . wait a minute . . . I got the heart pain again . . . somedays it won't stop . . ."

Heddy-Anna's friends, impatient to resume partying, began to signal her to hang up the phone.

She nodded. "I can't talk anymore," she whined, "I'm short of breath. I need my rest. I can't believe you're calling so late. But what do I expect from sons who never come to see their mama?"

"Mama, you *know* how much we love you," Eddie sobbed.

A click in his ear was her response.

Jewel handed Eddie a fresh handkerchief. Junior blew his nose vigorously.

Marge and Charlie looked appropriately grave. Marge stood up. "I'm so sorry I said anything. I just thought it might be better to let you know, in case you wanted to go spend the holidays with her."

Charlie looked embarrassed. "Marge, would you wait in the car please? There's a little business I have to discuss with Junior and Eddie."

"Of course." Marge grabbed Junior's hand and pressed it. "I'm so sorry," she mouthed.

As she passed Eddie, she kissed him comfortingly on the cheek.

"Walk Marge to the car, Jewel, and then give us a few minutes," Junior ordered.

Jewel linked her arm with Marge. "Come on, honey. You were just trying to help."

When they were out of earshot, Charlie said hesitantly, "Of course, you understand that Marge is under the impression that you've visited Mama Heddy-Anna regularly over the years."

"It's a good thing she understands that," Junior snapped.

Charlie let it pass. "I felt so upset when Marge told me about her dream. Knowing the circumstances, something occurred to me. It may be a wild idea, but . . ." He paused and shrugged. "Well, at least I want you to know about it. It's a way that just might make it possible for you to safely visit your mother on Christmas Eve."

"What are you talking about?" Junior demanded.

"What does the St. Stephen of the Mountains monastery mean to you?"

"St. Stephen of the Mountains monastery? That was in the next town from us, just over the border. We used to ski there all the time when we were kids. It's been shut down since before we left."

"I thought you might have heard about it. They're reopening the monastery as a hotel on New Year's Day."

"No kidding." Eddie blinked. "Nobody was ever allowed in there. But what about it anyhow?"

"My cousin, who is a nun, usually joins us for Christmas dinner. She won't be with us this year because she's going on a pilgrimage. Sixty nuns and brothers and priests from all over the country will be staying at St. Stephen's during Christmas week, before it opens to the public."

They're getting the message, Charlie thought, as he saw the brothers exchange thoughtful glances. "They've chartered a plane that is leaving tomorrow evening from Teterboro Airport in New Jersey. They'll land at the new airstrip near the hotel, which, of course, is just over the border from your mother's home."

Charlie hesitated, wishing he could mop his brow, but he didn't want to seem nervous.

"I asked my cousin if there were any seats left on the charter, and as of this morning there still were four or five."

Junior and Eddie looked at each other. "We could ski from the monastery to Mama's house in no time at all," Eddie said.

Charlie swallowed, aware he either was about to hit a home run, or strike out. "I was thinking that if you two dressed as monks who had taken the vow of silence, there'd be no danger of anyone finding out who you are. I imagine you could easily arrange for the proper documentation."

"No problem," Junior said brusquely. There was a pause. He looked at his brother. "It always seemed too risky to go back home, but this could work."

"I'm going back," Eddie said, determination in his voice. "I'd never close an eye if anything happened to Mama before I got to see her again."

Charlie frowned. "We're going to have to act fast. The seats may already be gone."

"They better not be." Junior glowered. "When you heard about them, you shudda told us right away."

Charlie took out his cell phone.

"No, call from our phone. Put it on the speaker," Junior ordered.

"Of course."

"St. Mary's Convent," a woman's voice answered softly. "Sister Joseph speaking."

"Sister Joseph, this is Charles Santoli, Sister Margaret's cousin."

"Yes, how are you Mr. Santoli?"

"I'm well. Is Sister Margaret there?"

"No, I'm sorry, she's doing some last-minute shopping for her trip. We were advised to bring extra sweaters or wraps."

The brothers looked at Charlie. "Ask her," Junior said impatiently.

"Sister, do you happen to know if the flight to St. Stephen's is full?"

"I think it is, but let me take a look."

"There's *gotta* be room," Eddie whispered, clenching and unclenching his hands.

"I'm back, Mr. Santoli. I was right. We were full, but we just had two cancellations. One of our elderly sisters isn't well enough to make the long flight, so she and her companion are staying home."

"She better not have a quick recovery," Junior growled. "Book us those two seats."

On the other end of the phone, FBI agent Susan White, who had been sitting in the convent for several hours, waiting for the call, gave a thumbs-up to Rich Meyers.

Then she began to write, "Brother Stanislas and Brother Casper . . ."

Marge and Charlie were marvelous, Sterling thought, smiling from ear to ear as he realized that the first phase of the plan had worked perfectly.

Marissa, we're getting there, he thought.

"Good night, Marissa," Denise said, as she tucked her daughter in and bent down to give her a kiss.

"Good night, Mommy. I can't wait to wake up tomorrow. It's my birthday *and* it's Christmas Eve."

"We're going to have *lots* of fun," Denise promised as she turned out the light.

Downstairs, she joined Roy, who was drying the pots. "Everybody bedded down?" he asked cheerfully.

"Yes, but it's strange. I thought Marissa would be upset tonight, but she seems to be excited and happy, as though she's expecting a miracle, as though Billy and Nor will be here tomorrow."

"Then she's in for a terrible letdown," Roy said mournfully as he folded the dish towel.

"I got them everything they need," Charlie fretted. "The monks' habits, the sandals, the prayer books, the suitcases—real beat-up ones, like the brothers took the vow of poverty and meant it."

He and Marge and Sterling were sitting in the Santolis' living room, all of them tense with concern that the Badgett brothers would smell a rat before the pilgrimage charter plane took off.

"How about their passports?" Marge asked. "Any chance of a glitch with them?"

"First-rate forgeries," Charlie said. "They took care of that themselves."

"How were they getting to Teterboro?" Marge asked nervously. "I hope they didn't go in that showy limo."

"They were having the limo drive them to New York to one of their dry-cleaning shops that was closed. They were going to change there and take one of those cheap car services to the airport."

It was 11:55. The plane was due to take off at midnight.

"I don't know. Those two have a sixth sense," Charlie

moaned. "If at the last minute they figure out this was a setup, and don't get on that plane, I'm dead."

"Did you pick up any indication that they were suspicious when you saw them earlier today?" Marge asked, nervously shredding a cocktail napkin.

"None. I'm their new best friend. Don't forget, I'm the one who's getting them home to see Mama."

If this doesn't work, I'm the one who gets blamed for suggesting it, Sterling thought with a pang of guilt.

The ring of the phone made everyone jump.

Charlie grabbed the receiver. "Hello."

"Mr. Santoli?"

"Yes."

"This is Rich Meyers. You'll be glad to hear that a certain charter plane has just taken off, with Brothers Stanislas and Casper on board."

Charlie's relieved smile told Marge and Sterling what they needed to know.

"They should be landing in Wallonia in eight hours. The police there are waiting to arrest them. Our agents on board will shed their clerical robes and ride back home as soon as the plane refuels."

Charlie felt as though a two-ton weight had been lifted from his shoulders. "I imagine you'll want to be taking further statements from me."

"Next week. Enjoy your holiday. I know you'll cooperate with us." Meyers paused. "Don't worry too much, Mr. Santoli. I think you know what I mean."

"Thank you," Charlie said quietly.

Sterling stood up. "It's going to be okay," he said. "You're going to be fine, Charlie. You're a good man. And now I must leave you."

"Sterling, how can we ever thank you?" Marge asked.

"Don't even think about thanking me. Just use your time on earth wisely. Believe me, it goes very quickly."

Marge and Charlie entwined their hands. "We'll never forget you," Marge whispered.

"Never," Charlie echoed fervently.

"We'll meet again. I'm very sure of that," Sterling said as he disappeared.

"How much longer? This robe is making me itch," Eddie hissed, and was rewarded by an elbow in the ribs from Junior.

Junior fished a pad from his pocket and wrote, "Vow of silence. Shut up. Almost there."

At that moment the voice of the flight attendant came over the loudspeaker. "We are due to land at Monastery Airport in twenty minutes . . ." The usual instructions followed.

Eddie was twitching with excitement and beside himself with joy. Mama Heddy-Anna! I'm coming, Mama! he thought.

Junior didn't know the exact moment when the sinking feeling started. He looked out the window and narrowed his eyes. It was cloudy and, as the plane began to descend, light snow drifted against the windows.

He craned his neck and narrowed his eyes then spotted the monastery and the landing strip next to it. It's okay, he thought. For a minute I had a feeling that Santoli mighta skunked us.

Then the voice of the flight attendant came on again. "We have just been advised that due to extremely icy conditions, we will be unable to land at Monastery airport. Instead we will be landing at Wallonia City airport thirty miles away."

Junior and Eddie looked at each other. Eddie pushed back the hood of his robe. "Whaddaya think?"

SHUT UP, Junior scribbled furiously.

"You will be bussed immediately to St. Stephen's Monastery," the flight attendant chirped happily. "We do regret this inconvenience, but your safety is our first concern."

"How do we go through customs?" Eddie was trying unsuccessfully to whisper. "Are the passports okay if they really look at them under a special light or something?"

SHUT UP, Junior scrawled. Maybe it's okay, he thought. Maybe it's on the level. He looked around, searching out the faces of his fellow passengers. Most of them were deep in their prayer books.

THE PASSPORTS ARE OKAY, he wrote. IT'S YOUR BIG MOUTH I'M WORRYING ABOUT.

Eddie leaned over him to look out the window. "We're over the mountain. Look! There's the village. Look! I bet I can pick out Mama's house."

His voice was rising. To cover the sound, Junior began to cough violently. Immediately the hostess was at his side offering water.

I need a drink, he thought wildly. If we get back to Long Island, I'll tear Charlie Santoli apart limb from limb.

The plane landed, taxiing to a halt a good distance from

the terminal. What Junior and Eddie saw out on the tarmac rendered them both more speechless than any vow of silence could ever have accomplished.

In the midst of dozens of uniformed Wallonian policemen, a lone figure was jumping up and down and waving vigorously.

Mama Heddy-Anna.

Junior shook his head. "She don't look like she's dying to me."

Eddie's face was puzzled. "She looks so healthy. I can't believe it."

"We took this trip for nuthin', and now we're gonna spend the rest of our lives in jail."

The door of the plane opened and four policemen raced down the aisle. Junior and Eddie were encouraged to get out of their seats and put their hands behind their backs. As they were led away, their fellow passengers began removing roman collars and nun's veils, and burst into spontaneous applause.

At the foot of the stairs, they were enveloped in one of Mama Heddy-Anna's bear hugs.

"The nice policemen came for me. They said you were coming home as a surprise. I know you're in trouble, but good news! Papa was just made head trustee at the prison where you'll be staying from now on." She beamed, "All three of my boys together, nice and safe, where I can visit every week."

"Mama," Eddie sobbed as he laid his head on her shoulder. "I been so worried about you the whole time I was gone. How do you feel?"

Heddy-Anna patted him. "Never better."

Junior thought of the estate on Long Island, the limo, the money, the power, and Jewel, whom he knew would have a new boyfriend in two weeks. As Eddie's shoulders shook with emotion, all Junior could think was, How could I have been so stupid?

On Christmas Eve morning, Billy and Nor were lingering over the breakfast neither one of them had any interest in touching. The distracting reality that it was both Christmas Eve and Marissa's eighth birthday hung over them, a dense, oppressive blanket of pain.

The sudden steady ring of the doorbell startled both of them. Billy ran to answer it.

A beaming Marshall Frank Smith boomed, "Grab only what you need. You're booked on the 12:40 flight to New York, and if you want to catch it, you haven't got a minute to spare."

On Christmas Eve, Nor's Place usually enjoyed a pleasant flow of lunch customers. Some were last-minute shoppers, stopping for a quick bite. Others, more organized, came in for a quiet lunch before the religious and family celebrations began.

Today this place feels downright eerie, Dennis thought, as he surveyed the room from behind the bar. He shook his head. At least Nor had agreed that it was pointless to stay open on Christmas Day.

"I guess you're right, Dennis," she had admitted. "Only ten reservations! Those people would be better off at a place with a little life in it."

We're pretty much at the end of the line here, Dennis thought, as he was handed an order for a single beer.

Just then the bar phone rang. He picked it up.

"Dennis!" It was Nor's voice, buoyant and energetic. "We're at the airport, on our way home. We're in the clear. The Badgett brothers are gone, locked up for good," she exulted. "Get a birthday cake for Marissa for tonight, and phone our usual Christmas people. Tell them Nor's Place will be open for Christmas dinner and it's on the house. But don't let Marissa know! We want to surprise her."

From the moment she opened her eyes on Christmas Eve and whispered to herself, "Today I am eight years old," Marissa began to lose faith that Sterling would be able to bring Daddy and NorNor home. She had been sure they would be there when she woke up, but now she realized it was going to be like all the other times.

She had promised herself they would be back for Easter, but they weren't. Then she had been sure they'd be home when school closed for the summer . . . Then when it opened in September . . . Then for Thanksgiving . . .

It's going to be just like that again today, she thought, as she got up and put on her bathrobe. Tears kept trying to flow from her eyes, but she pressed them back with her hands. Trying to put a smile on her face, she went downstairs.

Her mother and Roy and the twins were already at the kitchen table. They all began to sing "Happy Birthday" when they saw her. There were presents next to her cereal bowl: a new watch; books and CDs from Mommy and Roy and the twins; a sweater from Grandma. Then she opened the last two boxes: ice skates from Daddy and a new skating outfit from NorNor.

Now she was absolutely, positively sure they wouldn't be

coming home today. If they were, wouldn't they wait to give her the presents when she saw them?

After breakfast Marissa carried all her gifts upstairs. When she reached her room, she dragged the chair from her desk over to the closet and stood up on it. She lifted the boxes with the new ice skates and the skating outfit and put them on the top shelf. Then, with the tips of her fingers, she pushed them back as far as she could, until they were out of sight.

She never wanted to look at them again.

At eleven o'clock she was in the living room, reading one of her new books, when the phone rang. Even though her heart stopped when she heard Mommy say, "Hello, Billy," she still didn't look up.

But then Mommy came rushing over to her. She didn't give her a chance to say, "I don't want to talk to Daddy," before the phone was at her ear and Daddy was shouting, "Rissa, want to go to Nor's Place for your birthday dinner? We're on the way home!"

Marissa whispered, "Oh, Daddy." She was bursting with so much happiness that she couldn't say anything more. And then she felt someone pat the top of her head. She looked up and there he was—her friend who wore the funny hat and who was not quite an angel, and he was smiling at her.

"Good-bye, Marissa," he said, and then he was gone.

In a daze, Marissa climbed the stairs to her room, closed the door, pulled over her chair, and stood on her tiptoes to retrieve the presents she had pushed away. But when she pulled the boxes down, something fell from the shelf and landed at her feet.

She sank to the floor and stared at the tiny Christmas ornament that she had never seen before. It was an angel dressed just like her friend.

"You've got the same funny hat," she whispered as she picked it up and kissed it. Holding it to her cheek, she looked out the window and up at the sky.

"You told me you weren't quite an angel," she said softly. "But I know that you are. Thank you for keeping your promise to help me. I love you."

When Sterling entered the celestial conference room of the Heavenly Council and saw the approving looks on the faces of the saints, he knew he had completed his task to their satisfaction.

"I say, that was most touching," the admiral said with uncharacteristic tenderness.

"Did you see that child's face?" The nun sighed. "It shone with as perfect happiness as is possible on earth."

"I couldn't help staying until I saw Marissa in her father's arms," Sterling explained to the council. "Then I went back to Nor's Place with them. What a wonderful birthday party it was. As you know, the word that they'd returned flashed all over town, and everyone came in to welcome them home."

"I had tears in my eyes when Billy sang the song he wrote for Marissa," the queen observed.

"Talk about a sure-fire hit," the matador declared.

"As you know, he'll be recording it and the other songs he wrote while he was away," Sterling said. "It was a very painful year for him, but he used it well."

"As did you," the shepherd said quietly.

"Yes indeed. Absolutely," they all murmured, nodding.

"You not only found someone to help and used your head to work out a solution to her problem, but you also used your heart," the Native American saint said, clearly proud of Sterling.

"And you saved Charlie Santoli from the destructive life he was leading," the nun added.

There was a pause.

Then the monk stood up. "Sterling, the celebration of the birth of our Savior is about to begin. It is the judgment of the council that you have earned not only a visit to heaven, but your permanent place there. It is time for us to lead you through the gates." He turned toward the door.

"Wait a minute," Sterling said. "I have something to ask you."

The monk stared at him. "What could you possibly have to ask at this moment?"

"I am so grateful to all of you. As you know, I long to be in heaven. But I so enjoyed this experience that, by your leave, I would like to return to earth every Christmas and find someone who needs help. I never knew how good it could feel to really make a difference in other people's lives."

"Making other people happy is one of the great joys of the human condition," the monk told him. "You have learned your lesson even better than we realized. And now, come along."

✶

As they approached, the heavenly gates opened wide before them, revealing a light brighter than a thousand suns, brighter than anything that Sterling had ever been able to imagine. A profound inner peace permeated his being. He was going toward the light; he was part of the light. The Heavenly Council stepped aside, and slowly and reverently he continued to walk forward. He was aware that there was one large group of people who were gathered together.

He felt a hand touch his. "Sterling, let me walk with you."

It was Annie.

"The other newcomers are just ahead of you," she whispered. "They all came together. Their lives ended tragically, and although they themselves have found eternal joy, they are deeply concerned for the loved ones they left behind. But they will find their own ways to send help and comfort to them."

Annie paused. "Oh listen, the celebration is beginning."

Music filled the air, rose toward a crescendo. With the angels and saints and all the other souls in heaven, Sterling lifted his voice in song as they continued walking toward the light.

"*Glory to the newborn King . . .* "